THE THREE GOLD DOUBLOONS

BY EDITH THACHER HURD

Cover design by Elle Staples

Cover illustration by Larissa Sharina

Inside illustrations by Clement Hurd

© 2018 Jenny Phillips

www.jennyphillips.com

Originally published in 1954 under the title *The Devil's Tail*.

More Books from The Good and the Beautiful Library!

His Indian Brother
by Hazel Wilson

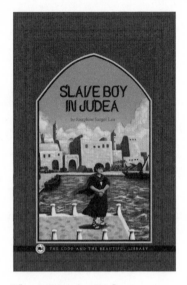

Slave Boy in Judea
by Josephine Sanger Lau

Zeke and the Fisher-Cat
by Virginia Frances Voight

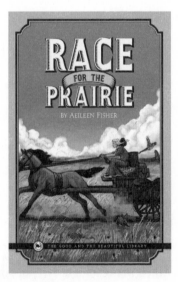

Race for the Prairie
by Aileen Fisher

TABLE OF CONTENTS

CHAPTER 1

Tom shivered a little as he walked. It was the first day of the new year, 1775, and even a buckskin jacket and long leather breeches offered little protection against the sharp January winds. The red clay of the road had frozen into thin ruts that made walking painful in soft leather moccasins.

Stopping a moment, Tom closed his eyes against a spat of white snow swirling out of the cold sky. As he stood, he listened. He listened to the endless sighing of the tall pines through which the road had been cut. He listened to the sound of the snow sputtering against the buckskin of his jacket, and he listened to the silence. Suddenly, now that he had only a little farther to go, Tom was afraid. Deep down inside of him was a new sort of fear that he had never known before, not the kind of fear that crept over you when you were lost in the woods at night and couldn't tell which way to turn. No, nor the kind of fear you had all alone in a cabin when the lightning tore out of the mountains and smashed across the valley, jabbing at the trees in great yellow streaks.

"I almost wish I hadn't come," he thought as he turned once more to face the cutting wind. "I wish I'd stayed home. How am I ever going to get used to living in a town, to wearing the funny clothes they do, to not carrying a gun, and those stiff shoes?"

Suddenly, Tom knew what was the matter. He knew all right, but he didn't like to admit it even to himself. He missed his ma. He was homesick even though he was fifteen and had been away from home only four days. He couldn't help it. Right now Williamsburg seemed a mighty long way from Frederick County.

Wiping his cold hand across his mouth, Tom swallowed hard and took a firmer grip on the stick holding his little bundle of possessions. Then he broke into a dog-trot. He had gone barely a mile when suddenly, looking ahead, he saw it. There it was. He could just make out the shapes, the fences, and the already tiny spots of light showing through the gray winter darkness.

"Williamsburg!" Tom whispered aloud as he stopped. "Williamsburg." He said the name almost reverentially. Would it truly be his home from now on? Tom felt a heavy pounding inside of him as he hurried forward once more. It was not long before he came to a small sandy path running beside a wooden fence. Inside the fence stood several red brick buildings.

"Must be the college," thought Tom. "Must be William and Mary, 'cause Mr. Thruston told me that would be the first thing I'd come to. 'It's the college at one end of the town and the Capitol at the other, Tom,' he had said. 'And, coming in from the mountains as you will, you'll see the college buildings first.'"

Tom was soon at the gates. He stood looking in. Directly in front of him at the end of a long walk stood a large red brick building more beautiful than anything Tom had ever seen in his whole life. It was topped by a high cupola, and along the front ran a double row of windows, from each of which glimmered a small spot of yellow light. On either side of this main building were two others, smaller, but equally elegant, it seemed to Tom as he stood wondering which Mr. Thruston had told him was the school for the Indian boys.

Too lost in admiration and too absorbed trying to recall all that he had read of the great men and students who were fortunate enough to study and teach here, Tom paid little heed to the hubbub of voices and clatter of horses' hoofs and carriage wheels that kept up continuously behind him on the main street of the town. Suddenly there came a "Holla. Clear the way."

Tom jumped and threw himself safely out of the way, waiting until the heavy, pounding hoofs had passed. Then he turned. Angrily he looked after the fast-disappearing carriage. Through the dusk he could just make out an arrogant figure sitting erect as a musket in the high seat, the reins held tightly in his hands, while the woman beside him looked neither to right nor left.

There came a whimper, a short growl, and Tom saw

something white sprawled in the frozen road before him. Dropping his bundle, he ran forward. A small white dog lay on its side where the carriage had passed. Tom knelt down and, with strong, tender fingers, felt the little creature all over.

"You're not really hurt," he half whispered as he stroked the long white hair back from the little black eyes. "He may have hit you, but he did you no harm."

Then Tom lifted the dog in his arms, and as he stood up, he saw for the first time the large group of people gathered about him. There was anger and resentment in the faces, and Tom's unasked question was answered by a mountain of a man whom Tom took to be a blacksmith, for he wore a great leather apron over his jacket.

"It's our Governor, boy. You must have just come to Williamsburg, or else you'd know better than to be caught even on the sidewalk when His Lordship is out driving."

"Eh," a young dandy beside him agreed. "But what horses, my friend. Beautiful, beautiful! If one must be run down, at least let us have the Governor's best."

There was a roar of laughter as the dandy stopped speaking. Tom stood bewildered. He did not understand the laughter. Was he being made the laughingstock of them all? Or was this just the manner in which city folk joked with each other? A hot flush of anger spread over his face. He felt his grip tighten on the small dog in his arms. But before he could think how to address the young man, the crowd seemed to melt into the darkness as abruptly and quietly as they had collected, leaving Tom angry and alone in the strange city.

CHAPTER 2

"Then you are a newcomer?"

Tom whirled, for he had not heard anyone come up to him. The man repeated his question as he saw the surprised look on Tom's face.

"Eh," Tom answered gruffly, determined not to allow himself to be laughed at again. "I've just come. A fine welcome your governor gave me, almost running me down and trampling on this little dog without even stopping to see what damage he'd done."

The man, who seemed to Tom to be standing almost too close to him now, smiled a queer, crooked smile that looked hardly a smile at all, more the mere twisting of the thin, pale lips.

"That's right, boy, Lord Dunmore doesn't care much for us, nor we for him, for that matter. The king sent him to whip our colony back into obedience, but he's not succeeding too well."

Once more the lips twisted, and this time Tom looked more closely at the sharp nose, the deep-set eyes, and the narrow little chin down which ran a deep cleft that looked as if it had been molded of soft clay. The man's clothes were elegant, but since he was standing so close, it was not hard for Tom to see that, despite their elegance, they were threadbare at the cuffs, and there were spots on the waistcoat.

After a moment of silence between the two, Tom, remembering that he had as yet no place to spend the night, asked questioningly:

"I wonder, sir, that is—do you by any chance know a certain Mr. Purdie? Mr. Alexander Purdie, sir. He is a printer. His business is with Mr. Hunter and Mr. Dixon, whom, I believe, are the printers of the Virginia Gazette."

"Indeed," the stranger said in a low, half-whispering voice. "We all know the good Mr. Purdie, but may I correct you. He is no longer in business with Hunter and Dixon, for scarcely a month ago he set up his own shop. I have heard it rumored that he did not agree with his two partners in this trouble we are having with the king."

Tom's heart sank. Perhaps now that he was in business for himself, Mr. Purdie would not want an apprentice. Perhaps his business would be too small to need any help. Or even more likely, he already had all the helpers he could employ. Tom had dreamed so long of becoming a printer and being allowed to work on the Virginia Gazette, and now—now perhaps there would be no place for him at all.

"He doesn't even publish the Gazette, then?" he burst out miserably.

"Not yet, boy," the stranger answered, somewhat puzzled by Tom's unhappiness. "But I have no doubt he will eventually. In fact, I believe he has already announced such an intention as soon as he gets himself squared away in the new shop. That will give us three Virginia gazettes here in Williamsburg, all blowing away as hard as they can every week."

Tom gasped. "Three gazettes!"

"Eh," the older man answered, cocking his three-cornered hat well over his left eye. "There's Mr. Hunter and Dixon's; there's Mr. Pinkney's—he took over from Mrs. Rind—and soon there will be Mr. Purdie's."

As he spoke, the man made a motion to take Tom by the arm. There was a weak growl. Tom looked down in surprise. The little dog that had, up until this moment, lain quietly in his arms, moved uneasily. Tom could feel her body go tense now.

"Ugly rascal." The stranger withdrew his hand. Tom was puzzled. The man seemed friendly enough, and the dog had not objected to Tom picking her up and holding her, yet she would not let this stranger so much as touch Tom's arm. What did she sense that Tom did not? He puzzled over this as he walked back to pick up his small bundle of possessions that he had dropped at the edge of the street when he hurried to the little dog.

"Come, boy." The stranger followed after him. "I'll show you Mr. Purdie myself. I'll be going that way, for I've decided that the two of us must seal our friendship in a tankard of ale at the Raleigh. It is most opposite Mr. Purdie's at the other end of the Duke of Gloucester Street."

"You mean, sir"—Tom hesitated—"that you would like me to drink ale with you at the Raleigh Tavern?"

Tom remembered that the men who used to come from

Williamsburg to talk to his father about the lands to the west spoke often of the Raleigh—the good food, fine company, and happy time to be had there. Indeed, many said it was the finest hostelry in all of Virginia.

"That's just what I mean, boy." The man chuckled hoarsely. "We'll stop there, you and I, and you can tell me more about yourself."

Tom was silent a moment, thinking. Indeed, he would have liked nothing better than to see the inside of so famous an ordinary, but he knew full well his ma had told him that, above all things, he was not to take spiritous liquors of any kind. He'd never been allowed them at home, and he was not to start drinking them when away.

"No, please, sir, if you don't mind. I'd rather go directly to Mr. Purdie's. It's getting late, and perhaps he will not admit me, even though I do carry the letter from Mr. Thruston."

"Mr. Thruston?" questioned the stranger.

"Eh, he's the rector of the Frederick Parish, and he's the one who sent me to seek employment of Mr. Purdie. Mr. Thruston taught me to read and write, sir. Even some Greek and Latin," Tom added proudly.

"I see." Tom wondered if there was a touch of sarcasm in his friend's voice. "So you've come to Williamsburg to be apprenticed to Mr. Purdie."

"That's right, sir," Tom answered eagerly. "I want to be a printer. I've read a lot about Mr. Benjamin Franklin, and I want to be like him. I'd like to be the best printer in all of Virginia someday."

"Hmm. A worthy ambition indeed, my boy."

Once more Tom wondered if this strange man who seemed to be so friendly could perhaps also be laughing at him. He felt embarrassed now to have spoken so freely of his deepest desire to a complete stranger.

"Of course, I know it takes a long time to learn the trade, but I'm willing to work," he added quickly, hoping to sound less like an eager child and more like the man he was trying so hard to appear.

While they talked, the man had steered Tom across the street, dodging carefully between the carriages and chariots with their coachmen bellowing and cracking their whips as they passed one another. He chatted on as they walked slowly together down the sandy path by the side of the street, but Tom no more heard him than if he had been a magpie in one of the great trees that lined the beautiful street. This is what Tom had dreamed of. This was what Mr. Thruston had told him about: the white houses set back from the street, neat picket fences that gave a glimpse of the gardens behind them, and the box hedges now covered with a dusting of white snow spread over their dark leaves.

"Oh, sir," Tom broke in on the chatter of his companion, "that across the street—" he said, pointing, "that church, surely it must be Bruton Parish Church?"

"And indeed it is, my boy." The stranger looked down at Tom. "Your friend, Mr. Thruston, seems to have drilled you well on this town."

"He did, sir. After we finished our lessons at night, he would talk of the days he had spent here and of the beauties of the place, but of course, Bruton Parish Church meant more to him than any other building."

"Yes, yes." The stranger seemed anxious not to linger too long in the vicinity of the church; whereas, Tom would have liked to cross the street and get a better look within the high brick walls that half concealed the main part of the building. But he could feel the man was anxious to move on.

"And that, my boy, is the Governor's Palace." Tom's companion pointed down the long green that stretched at right angles to the main thoroughfare. Tom, looking eagerly, saw the most beautiful, the most elegant building he had ever imagined. The red bricks fairly glowed in the late afternoon grayness. Lights flickered from the many tall windows, and huge gates stood at the entrance like proud sentinels.

"It's—it's sort of different from the log houses we have back in Frederick County," Tom explained as he realized that he had been standing gaping for several minutes.

"Yes." Tom looked up to see the strange, crooked smile playing once more against the stranger's thin lips. "Eh, it's fine enough, about the finest building in the whole of the colony, and, by gad, we've had some mighty fine governors living there, too. Not like this haughty fool, Dunmore. But come, it's getting late, and I can see the lamp-lighter coming up the street. Come—" The man hesitated a minute. "What shall I call you?"

"Tom Cartwright," Tom answered boldly, for his father, when he lived, had always taught him to answer up. Tom could hear the strong voice even now. "Cartwright's a name to be proud of," he would say. "Speak up when you're asked for it."

"Um, Tom Cartwright." The stranger seemed to be turning the name over in his mind.

"And yours, sir?" Tom asked.

The other started at Tom's question. He hesitated as if considering. "Valentine." He spoke slowly. "My name is Valentine."

"Valentine?" queried Tom. "You mean, Mr. Valentine?"

"No"—the man hesitated—"yes, yes, of course, Tom. Call me Mr. Valentine if you please."

Suddenly he stopped, touched Tom on the arm, and pointed to a small shop in front of which they were now standing.

"If you will look closely, Tom, you will see the good Mr. Purdie himself and his elegant son, James— the father working, the son idling as usual."

Tom took a step forward and looked eagerly in through the large window facing the street. By the light of a spreading chandelier, he could see a heavyset figure seated on a high stool before a square tray of type. With his back to the window stood a tall boy. His hands moved. His shoulders rose and fell, and his head moved jerkily as if to emphasize what he was saying to the older man. Tom could not help stepping closer. It was hard to make out much more of the shop in the sparse candlelight, but at the far end, there was no mistaking the two great presses, their handles like great wooden tails protruding into the shadows of the room.

"It is too bad to arrive cold and half-starved at your new employer's." Mr. Valentine spoke hurriedly. "Come, will you not join me at the Raleigh?"

Looking across the street to where his companion pointed, Tom saw a brightly lighted building considerably larger than most on the street. Outside the door many horses were tied. Servant boys hustled in and out, holding reins for gentlemen and giving assistance to those who drove up in their carriages. It was a busy place, indeed, and Tom would have liked to accompany his friend, but now that he had once seen Mr. Purdie, nothing would have persuaded him to go past the shop without presenting his letter.

"Oh, no, no, Mr. Valentine, thank you. But I must go to Mr. Purdie. It is getting late, and I truly must find myself lodgings if Mr. Purdie will not have me. But will you not come in with me, since you seem to know Mr. Purdie?"

"Me?" Mr. Valentine fairly jumped at the very idea of entering the print shop. "Me?" he repeated nervously. "Certainly not."

Then, before Tom had a chance to urge him further or even to thank him for his kindness, the man vanished into the night.

Tom hesitated a moment. Then, taking a firm grip on his stick and tucking the little dog more comfortably under his arm, he walked deliberately up the steps and rapped on the printing office door.

CHAPTER 3

Tom felt his heart pounding inside of him as Mr. Purdie looked up. Shielding his eyes from the candlelight, he peered into the darkness outside.

"Who's there? Come in." The voice sounded questioning but not unfriendly.

Lifting the iron latch, Tom stepped into the shop. It was warm inside, with the strong smell of fresh printer's ink. The boy who had been talking with such vigor turned as Tom entered. Tom recognized him immediately as the dandy who had made the remark about the governor's horses a short while before.

"You are Mr. Purdie, sir?" Tom spoke hesitantly, trying hard to conceal his anxiety.

"Yes, I am. What is it you wish of me, boy?" The voice was so kindly and the manner so friendly that a sudden wave of relief swept over Tom. He seemed unable to speak for a moment. There was something so secure and honest about the quiet voice, the pleasant roll of the Scottish Rs, and the steady look of the blue eyes as they peered through the little metal-rimmed glasses. He was examining Tom from the matted fur of his cap to the mud on his worn moccasins.

Tom began slowly, "I come, sir, that is—I have come with a letter. It is a letter Mr. Thruston, Mr. Charles Myms Thruston, of Frederick County, wrote for me."

"Mr. Thruston! The Charles Myms Thruston?" Mr. Purdie exclaimed in delight. "But this is wonderful. Why, we knew him well when he was at Gloucester Parish. Often he'd come to Williamsburg, and we'd read together. His knowledge of books always delighted me, and I believe he often bought more books than he should have." Mr. Purdie chuckled in happy recollection.

While the older man had been talking, Tom dug the letter, somewhat crumpled and soiled now, out of his pocket.

Mr. Purdie, who was barely as tall as Tom but easily twice as round, came forward holding out his hand. He stood looking affectionately at the letter for a moment as if he recognized the handwriting of an old and beloved friend. Then he hesitated; a look of anxiety crossed his face.

"There's nothing the matter, is there, boy? No harm has come to our good friend, I trust?"

"Oh no, sir. No, it's about me," Tom reassured him quickly. "Mr. Thruston was in fine health when I left."

Mr. Purdie climbed back onto his high stool and, looking somewhat like an overgrown schoolboy, broke open the seal and began reading. His face grew serious and cheerful by turns as he finished each of the five long pages Mr. Thruston had taken such pains to write. Tom knew what it said in them. He knew how it told of his father's death—the terrible accident of the tree, and how it had fallen on the older Cartwright, crushing his chest.

Tom could hardly think about it to this day, more than a year after. The great strong man lying in such pain and not crying out. Then the breath coming slowly in short gasps. His calling to Tom, "It's no use, boy," he had said. "It's all over for me, Tom. Take care of your mother and the little one, Milly. God bless you, my son . . ." The voice had sunk to a whisper, and the great head, with its mass of white hair, had fallen back. Tom knew then that his father was dead.

There was a rustle of paper in the silence. Tom started out of his memories. Mr. Purdie was looking at him. Then he went back to his reading. As the only other person in the shop, the young dandy paid no attention to him at all, sitting slouched in a chair reading the Virginia Gazette. Tom stood silent, examining the shop as best he could in the dim candlelight. It was not a large room but was carefully and neatly arranged with the type cases in a square to the right of the door as you entered; and, to the left, shelves of leather-bound books reached almost to the ceiling. In front of these was a counter indicating that Mr. Purdie ran a small bookstore as well as a printing office. Tom looked at the two presses that stood one on each side of the shop.

"Will I ever learn how they work?" he thought. "They look as if they had a lot to 'em." At the very back were stacks of unprinted papers and overhead racks for drying the wet sheets. Pots of ink and lampblack stood in neat rows on a shelf beside the further press.

Once more the silence was broken by the crackling of the stiff paper on which Mr. Thruston's letter was written. Mr. Purdie refolded it carefully. Taking his small spectacles in his stubby, ink-stained fingers, he rubbed the glasses with a white linen handkerchief.

"So," he began, looking over the top of the type cases at Tom. "So your name is Tom Cartwright. You come seeking employment. Do you know, Tom, what work being apprenticed to a printer can mean? It is long hours, painstaking, careful work. And since I plan to publish another Gazette, which must be ready for our subscribers each Friday without fail, we will seldom have time to waste here."

Mr. Purdie replaced his now polished spectacles. Sliding his short legs off the high stool, he came around the cases and stood looking closely at Tom.

"Oh, sir." Tom could not restrain his eagerness, for all of a sudden he had a great fear that perhaps Mr. Purdie would not think he was serious about wanting to learn the printing trade. "Oh, Mr. Purdie, please, sir, I assure you that I am willing to work any length of time. I'm used to hard work and long hours, sir. That would not bother me. Oh, please, please, Mr. Purdie, I do so want—"

Mr. Purdie raised his hand. He turned and walked up and down the shop several times before speaking again.

"Mr. Thruston has told me all that in the letter, Tom. He assured me that you are not only a willing worker but also an intelligent one." Tom flushed at this unexpected compliment. "Would that there were more like you."

The older man's voice had a tone of unmistakable bitterness in it as he aimed his remark in the direction of the boy who still sat absorbed in the Gazette. Mr. Purdie, turning, faced

Tom squarely and spoke slowly. "Indeed, I'll take you, Tom. I'm glad to have you, not only because I would like to do what I can for any friend of Mr. Thruston, but you have come at just the right time. I have been trying to obtain a good apprentice or somebody to assist me ever since I left Mr. Dixon, but—by gad—the young men of today seem afraid to soil their hands with good printer's ink."

Taking a step toward the Gazette reader, he continued. "Even my own son James, here, has just been informing me that he considers it beneath him."

Tom stood bewildered by this sudden outburst of feeling. His face flushed with a strange sort of embarrassment that he did not quite understand. But young James seemed not the least upset by his father's evident anger. Rising slowly, he folded his paper with great deliberation and placed it neatly in his pocket. He yawned slightly, straightened his dapper brown wig, fixed his white sock in place, and threw a heavy overcoat over his shoulders.

He turned, walked to the door, addressing his father casually over his shoulder as he passed. "I feel sure, sir," he drawled, "I feel sure that this sturdy fellow from the backwoods, this honest tender of cattle, is used to far worse than printer's ink on his hands."

Tom was not responsible for what happened after that. His bundle crashed to the floor. The little dog squealed miserably as she scuttled behind the type shelves. Tom lunged. His fists clenched. His jaw set tight and angry. But James was too quick for him. Already half out of the door, he ducked nimbly. Then, leaping quickly down the three steps and waving his three-cornered hat at Tom, he grinned sarcastically as he disappeared around the corner.

CHAPTER 4

Tom stood confused and embarrassed, not daring to look at Mr. Purdie.

"I'm sorry, sir," he gulped at last. "I guess I just forgot I wasn't in Frederick County any longer; out there we don't let people insult us the way he's done twice tonight."

There was a deep chuckle. Tom looked up in surprise. The blue eyes behind the little spectacles were crinkled at the corners, and the wide mouth grinned for a moment. Then the stubby hand passed over the round face, and Mr. Purdie became serious.

"Twice?" he queried.

"Yes, well, you see, sir, it was when I first came. I almost got run over by the governor, and your son James, sir, gathered with some others when I picked up the little dog and made a joke of me by saying at least it was good to be trampled by such fine horses as the governor's."

Mr. Purdie turned, walked slowly back to his high stool and, clambering up, sat holding one knee, rocking slightly back and forth.

"Horses, horses, nothing is too good for a horse, according to my son." Mr. Purdie removed his glasses once more, and once more there was a gesture of weariness as he passed his hand over his face. He looked suddenly very tired.

"Yes," Tom thought to himself, "yes, tired so he's almost sick." Then he spoke up. "I'm sorry, sir. Please forgive me, Mr. Purdie, I know I've done wrong. This is no time to attack the son of the only friend I have in Williamsburg."

A sudden wave of deep homesickness passed over Tom as he spoke. Why, oh, why had he come? Why had he ever left home to get mixed up with these strange city folk? Mr. Purdie must have sensed how Tom felt, for, coming quickly around the cases, he stood beside him and spoke earnestly.

"You must not take it so hard, boy." His voice was gentle. "Of course you are right. You should not have lost your temper. Fighting and brawling are not looked on with favor in Williamsburg, but"—his deep chuckle soothed and comforted Tom—"if I ever saw a boy who deserved a good thrashing, that one is my son James."

He stopped, then added thoughtfully, "I don't know what ails that boy. He's a strange lad. Ever since his mother died and I married Miss Peachy, he seems to have turned against me. He's a great worry to me, Tom; I might just as well be honest with you. You have seen for yourself how he likes to play the dandy, dressing in expensive clothes that I am hard put to pay for. And his associates, most of them, like that ignorant blacksmith, are men that I would not allow in my house. But they know the horses, and I swear sometimes I'm truly afraid of what James might do to get money for the races."

There was a silence. Heavy furrows had come in the little man's forehead. Once more he looked tired and sick.

"But, but"—Mr. Purdie hesitated—"I guess I'm to blame also for what happened just now. I should not have chided him in front of you. I must warn you of one thing, Tom: James will never like you or forgive you if you come to work here for me. Although he does everything to defy me, still he's jealous of any attentions I show to others."

Once more Tom felt embarrassed. He had taken so violent a dislike to Mr. Purdie's son that it was almost impossible for him to say anything comforting to the older man.

"Don't worry for me, Mr. Purdie," he said gruffly at last. "I've always taken care of myself. I guess I can still."

Tom spoke with what he hoped was assurance, but inside there was a great loneliness and little of the confidence he boasted.

"Now, Tom." Mr. Purdie was suddenly all of a bustle. "We must not be late. Our evening meal comes early because of the younger boys, and old Betty, she's the cook, is a wildcat if we keep her good food waiting a minute."

"You mean, Mr. Purdie, that I am to come home with you tonight?"

Mr. Purdie, in the midst of removing his large apron, looked up in surprise. "But what else, boy? Do you have another place to go?"

"No, sir, I have not, but I was not quite sure if, as well as accepting me as your apprentice, you were also willing to take me into your home."

"Come, come, Tom." Again Mr. Purdie laughed a deep, comforting laugh. "You must indeed have formed a bad impression of city folk. To be honest, not only am I glad to have you as a friend of Mr. Thruston's, but it is also the duty of any master to provide food and lodgings for his apprentices.

Perhaps such a clause is even in the indenture which I will have you sign tomorrow. I'm not quite sure what it says, as Mr. Dixon always handled that side of the business, and as I said before, I have had no luck in the past month in finding anyone to serve me."

While he talked, Mr. Purdie had removed his apron, smoothed his brown wig, and put on his coat and great cloak. Taking his three-cornered hat from a peg on the wall, he snuffed out the candles in the chandelier. Then he motioned Tom to follow him as he opened the front door of the shop. Taking a key from his pocket, he turned to lock it. Suddenly there came a whimper.

"What's that?" Mr. Purdie looked up in surprise as the little white dog scuttled through the half-open door and down the steps to the sidewalk below.

Mr. Purdie scowled. "That dog, Tom," he said sharply, "it's not really yours, is it, boy?"

Tom hesitated, looking down at the little creature waiting eagerly for him at the bottom of the steps. "Well, sir—well, no, I suppose it isn't really. I only picked her up when she had almost been run over, but I don't suppose that really makes her my dog, does it?"

"Indeed not," Mr. Purdie answered firmly. "The town is full of stray dogs, so I would advise you to leave her alone. Let her run home, that is, if she has one."

Tom knew from the tone of the older man's voice that he must not protest further, no matter how much he wanted to keep the little dog. Descending the short flight of steps quickly, he deliberately avoided her and started up the street beside Mr. Purdie.

By now the lamps were lighted. Many of the houses still had their Christmas candles burning in the windows, throwing flickering shadows over the hedges and fences. Across the street there were more horses than before tied to the long bars outside the Raleigh Tavern, and the sound of chattering voices and gruff laughter could be heard halfway down the street. There were only occasional spatters of snow now, and the wind that had cut through Tom's buckskin jacket as he approached Williamsburg had died down. The little town seemed peaceful and, to Tom's eyes, hardly real with the neat houses, white fences, trimmed hedges, and orderly trees. There was a sense of security that seemed to pervade the very air, and Tom could not help thinking how different it all was from what he had been used to—the wild fields, the tall forests, and dark, wooded paths leading from one distant log house to another.

The people that they passed seemed to Tom so well fed, so cleanly and so elegantly dressed. He gaped openly, and they, in turn, looked quizzically at the young frontiersman accompanying Mr. Purdie. For his part, the latter was quite oblivious to these inquiring looks but hailed many friends as they walked the short distance from the printing office up the Duke of Gloucester Street to the Purdie house. Indeed, it seemed to Tom that his new master must know every person in Williamsburg, for he was constantly tipping his hat, wishing passersby a fine New Year, and stopping to exchange bits of news and gossip with most everyone he met. He slowed down as they approached a group of finely dressed men and women standing outside an elegant ordinary, before which swung a sign reading: The King's Arms.

"One of the best hostelries in town, Tom," Mr. Purdie explained. "Kept by Jane Vobe, very fine woman. Only the best clientele. Colonel George Washington, I feel sure you've heard of him even in Frederick County, always stays there when he takes his seat in the House of Burgesses. But here we are."

Mr. Purdie once more pulled a huge brass key from his seemingly bottomless pocket and hurried up a short flight of steps. Tom examined the house eagerly. It appeared larger than many in the town and different from most, in that it was built directly at the sidewalk with no fence or garden before it. A small porch with steps leading up to it from two sides sheltered the front door. From sparkling windows the cheerful glow of several candles shone down to light the sidewalk below.

Tom mounted the steps slowly, waiting for Mr. Purdie to unlock the door. But no sooner had the key turned and the door opened a crack than there came the scuffle of feet, and a small white object shot between Tom's legs. It twisted past Mr. Purdie on the doorstep, almost upsetting him, and disappeared into the house.

"Tom, get that nuisance out of here this minute, before she tracks mud all over the carpets. She's in the front room." Mr.

Purdie stepped back and fairly pushed Tom through the open door.

"Good heavens, Alexander, what's this? Is that you, Alexander?"

Tom hurried forward in the direction of the startled woman's voice, but he was not prepared for the opposition he was about to meet. No sooner had he entered the room indicated by Mr. Purdie than a small boy leapt forward waving his arms menacingly, while behind him another, who looked to Tom to be about ten years old, knelt beside the quivering little dog as if protecting her. The woman whose voice Tom heard in the hall had apparently risen very quickly from her high-backed chair beside the fire, for her needlepoint lay in a colorful heap on the floor.

Mr. Purdie hurried in, his three-cornered hat knocked to one side, his cloak half dragging from his shoulders.

"By gad, Tom, get that dog out of here! Did you hear me? Throw the tramp out the door."

"Oh, please, sir! Oh no, she's nice." The younger boy retreated slightly at the sight of his distracted father, but the elder son, holding the dog firmly in his arms, rose defiantly.

"No, you can't do that. She's cold. I like her."

"Alexander, please." The woman, her expression half puzzled, half laughing at the boys, turned pleadingly to Mr. Purdie. "What is this all about, Alexander?"

"I will explain later, Peachy, but right now, I want that dog removed from my house, Tom!"

Tom, taking a step forward, was immediately set upon by the younger of the two boys, who started pummeling him fiercely, then, grabbing him by the arm, bit him so hard that Tom cried out in pain and retreated. In doing so, he fell clumsily over a chair. A small vase with dried flowers was knocked from an end table, and in the midst of the confusion, the dog, apparently wishing to protect Tom, leaped from the older boy's lap and began barking furiously at Tom's attacker.

"Stop, stop, stop! For heaven's sake! Alex, William, put an end to this foolishness!" Mr. Purdie shouted wildly, clapping his hands. The younger son, whom Mr. Purdie had addressed as Alex, retreated from the dog's attacks behind Mrs. Purdie's full skirts. The older boy, William, picked up the angry little dog, and Tom, not knowing what else to do in his confusion, picked up the vase and flowers, doing his best to rearrange them once more.

"I think, Alexander," came the quiet voice of Mr. Purdie's wife, spreading a soothing calm over the general confusion, "I do think you owe us some sort of an explanation for such an unusual homecoming."

Perhaps to give himself time to regain his composure, and perhaps because he found it hard to answer his wife's gentle query without some harsh words, Mr. Purdie went back to the hall to remove his hat and cloak. Miss Peachy picked up her needlepoint and sat down once more by the fire. Tom, rubbing his sore arm miserably, retreated to the doorway, keeping a sharp eye on young Alex. As for the dog, she lay curled up once more in the older boy's lap looking quite innocent and as if she had no idea that she was the originator of all this confusion.

"Now, Alexander, what is all this about? Where did this little dog come from, and who, if I might ask, is this poor young man who has been so rudely set upon by your youngest son?"

There was something about the way the voice rose and fell

gently, the way the mouth curled up at the corners in a half smile, and the way the deep blue eyes twinkled as Miss Peachy finished speaking that made Tom wonder if this woman could ever really scold anyone. He liked her on the spot. And he thought he had never seen so pretty a dress, with its wide, flowing skirt and big, puffy sleeves. How well it was chosen to match the blue eyes and to go with the soft brown hair so neatly drawn back from Miss Peachy's round face. "How different from my mother's plain homespun," thought Tom. "It's quite easy to see she doesn't milk the cows in the winter or cut hay with the men in the summer." Tom couldn't help thinking this as he watched Miss Peachy's nimble white fingers making gay patterns on her needlework.

Miss Peachy smiled as Mr. Purdie reentered the room. He drew his large linen handkerchief from his pocket, removed his spectacles, and stood at the door, wiping the glasses with care. There was great silence in the room, broken only by the crackling of the fire.

CHAPTER 5

Mr. Purdie's good humor was soon restored, and Miss Peachy, on learning that Tom came as a friend of Mr. Thruston's, welcomed him as a new member of her family.

"You may sleep in James' room, Tom," she said, smiling. "That is"—Tom wondered if he noticed a quick look of anxiety pass over the good woman's face as she spoke of her husband's eldest son—"that is, until we can find some corner to give you as your own."

"Yes." Mr. Purdie spoke slowly. "Yes, Tom, I think the trundle in James' room is about the best we can do for you tonight. And now"—he glanced over at the large clock ticking quietly on the wall—"now it's almost time for us to sit down at the table, and perhaps you would like to get a bit of the hayseed out of your hair, eh, boy?" Mr. Purdie clapped Tom on the back with a low chuckle, and Miss Peachy motioned him to follow her up the stairs.

Once more Tom could not help but compare the elegance of this house into which he had been welcomed to the simple log cabin his father had hewn and built from the great trees of the forest. No rugs to cover the floor there, only the deep fur of a brown bearskin before the fire. There were no beautifully woven curtains at each window and no highly polished mahogany furniture, only the handmade chairs and rough pine table. As he followed Miss Peachy up the stairs, Tom spied gleaming silver laid on the dining room table, which was covered with a spotless linen cloth. In the bedroom to which Miss Peachy led him there was an air of brightness and cleanliness that Tom had never known before. No tired men kicked their mud-caked boots off on these soft rugs. No hands rough and sore from hours of wood chopping were washing in the elegant china washbasin that stood in one corner with its matching pitcher freshly filled with clean water.

Miss Peachy, on entering the room, which was lighted by several candles set about in highly polished brass candlesticks, went directly to the great bed that stood in one corner. Pulling back the red and white curtains, she began shaking whoever it was that had been asleep there.

"Wake up, James. Wake up, I say. I have brought your father's new apprentice to share your room with you at least for tonight."

Tom's heart sunk. Why must he be confronted with this boy at every turn? Why, oh why, couldn't he have been allowed to go to the stables to sleep with his dog and the horses? It would not have been the first time that he slept in straw with the farm animals, and he would have much preferred it to sharing anything at all with young James Purdie.

No sooner had the word apprentice been spoken than James, his black, close-cropped hair tousled and unbrushed, his small slit eyes squinting, and his face flushed the color of the red curtains, burst out of the bed.

"What! What!" he fairly screamed in rage. "That bumpkin, that backwoodsman, that tramp smelling of cow manure and no doubt crawling with lice, share my room? Indeed not."

Tom clenched his fists but did not move. He stood back to

allow Miss Peachy to handle her stepson. And this she did in a manner that Tom could not help but admire. For without the least hesitation, she stood directly over the boy and gave him a tongue-lashing and lesson in manners the like of which Tom had scarcely ever heard before. She called him a boor and a sloven who was not fit to share anybody's room as he neither worked nor cared to work. It was Tom, she ended with dignity, who might question perhaps if he would sleep in the same room as so worthless a creature. To Tom's amazement, James was silenced. Throwing himself back into his great double bed, he angrily jerked the curtain shut behind him.

"Now"—Miss Peachy turned back to Tom—"you may wash at the washstand over there. You see the clean towels, and I will have Alice make up the trundle later on." With that and not so much as a glance at the bed, she turned and walked out of the room, closing the door with a sharp little bang as she went.

Tom stood hesitating a moment, then he walked quietly to the great bed. "I'm sorry," he began. "I am sorry to bother you this way. I am sorry that you hate me for it. I mean you no harm." There was no sound at all from the curtain. Tom hesitated again, then continued, "Why do you hate me? What have I done to deserve so much scorn from you? I say again, I have not come here to cause trouble, only to learn a trade. Does it upset you so much that I should work for your father?"

Still there was no reply. This rudeness annoyed Tom. It took every bit of forgiveness he had to talk like this to someone who had treated him so badly, but he was determined to try and make a friend of James if he could. However, his good intentions were fast running out at the reception he was getting.

He could feel the anger mounting again and, turning from the bed, he threw his bundle on the table and began untying it.

He took out his clean shirt, so painstakingly washed and ironed by his mother the day before he left home. He half unwrapped the nightshirt she insisted he must wear in the city, although he had never had such a thing on his back since the day he was born. Then, stripping off his buckskin jacket, he stood naked to the waist, washing himself. Looking into the mirror which hung directly in front of him, Tom could not help smiling at the picture he presented. Nor could he quite blame James for calling him "hayseed" and "bumpkin," for his skin was rough and raw-looking from the days of walking in the winter wind. His brown hair was matted and unkempt, and even the brown freckles on his high cheekbones were scarcely visible through the dirt and grime on his face.

Tom stood grinning foolishly at himself in the gold-rimmed mirror. Suddenly the smile faded. Tom watched intently. The long curtains on the bed moved. They parted ever so slightly, and a white face peered out, watching him. Tom turned quickly, hoping to surprise James. But the curtains closed as silently as they had opened. Disgusted at such behavior and determined to steer a wide path around young Mr. Purdie from now on, Tom combed his hair as neatly as he could. Pulling his clean white shirt over his head, and walking quietly in his rough moccasins, he left the room without another word.

There was fried chicken and thick gravy. There were sweet potatoes cooked with almonds, corn fritters, black-eyed peas, and hot batter bread dripping with fresh butter. To end it all, there was one of old Betty's lemon cheesecakes for desert. When the meal was over, Tom was not sure if he could rise from the table or not. Never in his life had he ever dreamed of such food. Corn meal, pork and beans, tea, and in the summertime rough greens were all that he had been used to. That had always tasted good to him, but there was something so exciting about the thick chicken gravy, such mountains of hot bread, and the delicate sweetness of the cheesecake, that Tom wondered if he would ever be able to go back to his former rough fare.

Sitting about the fire with this friendly family, for James had never made an appearance, Tom could not help admitting that he had never been better fed, felt warmer, or been more comfortable in his entire life. It was indeed hard for him to believe that, at last, his dearest hopes and dreams were realized. He was really, in fact the very next day, to begin the work he had longed so often to be able to learn. Not only was he to be taught the trade which he most desired to know, but he was to be taught by a man whom he already liked so much. Tom felt at that moment that there could be no work too hard for him if Mr. Purdie were to ask him to do it.

As the family rose, Tom took a candle like the rest and mounted the stairs. The trundle was made up in James' room, but the curtains of the big bed were pulled open wide, and there was no sign of Tom's unhappy roommate. The sight of the clean linen sheets on the small trundle made Tom's bones fairly ache with the excitement of the last few days and long hours of walking. Going to the table where he had spread out his meager possessions, Tom picked up his nightshirt, determined to wear it tonight at least, as he had promised his anxious mother he would do. Unfolding it slowly, he waited for his small leather purse to fall out. He gave an impatient jerk. Then, shaking the nightshirt, he looked down at the floor, then back at the table, his eyes examining everything that was left there.

His purse. Where was it? His mother had given it to him as he started for Williamsburg. "Take care of it, Tom. Use only a little at a time," she had said. "It is half of all that your father was able to save for us. It is half of all the money that little Milly and I have in the world."

Tom could have sworn that he saw her wrap the purse carefully in his nightshirt, knowing that he would not unfold it until he was safely arrived in Williamsburg. He held the shirt high in the air and shook it violently. There was no mistaking the fact this time. His purse was not there.

CHAPTER 6

Tom's hands dropped to his sides. It took him several minutes to accept what he saw so clearly. His purse was gone!

Could it have slipped from his bundle? No, Tom felt that was impossible. Surely the handkerchief was tied too tightly. Then the only other person who might have seen it open was—James!

"Oh, no no no!" Tom whispered to himself. But he must have spoken more loudly than he realized, for there came a gentle voice from the doorway.

"Why, Tom," said Miss Peachy, "is something the matter? You sound so distressed."

There was no way out but to tell her. Tom tried to make as light of his loss as he could, but it was not hard for Miss Peachy to understand what this meant to him.

"You are sure, absolutely sure, Tom, that your mother put the purse in the nightshirt before she tied up the handkerchief?" Tom nodded. "But perhaps it fell out at one of the ordinaries at which you stopped."

"No, ma'am," Tom was forced to admit. "I'm afraid I didn't do much fixing up while I was coming. I kept what little money I needed in my jacket pocket and never opened my bundle at all the whole way."

Even in the candlelight Tom saw the look of troubled anxiety on Miss Peachy's face. Could it possibly be that she was also thinking, wondering about her stepson? Mr. Purdie's words in the shop came back to Tom now. "I'm truly afraid of what James may do to get money for the races." No, not Mr. Purdie's own son. He might be lazy and a dandy, but surely he was no thief.

Shaking each one carefully, Miss Peachy shuffled through Tom's scanty belongings on the table. Then she walked slowly around the table, stooping down to look under it. Finally she went deliberately to the bed and pulled back the red and white curtains. Picking up the pillows, she looked underneath them, and with this action, Tom knew for sure that his thoughts and hers were not far apart.

"I believe, Tom," Miss Peachy said thoughtfully, "It is best not to mention your loss to Mr. Purdie, or for that matter to anyone at all. There is still a chance that the purse fell out on the highroad, and we will make the proper inquiries tomorrow to retrieve it. Try to forget this sad thing that has happened and go to bed. You are tired and need rest after your long trip."

Tom was too weary to stay awake long, despite his sadness over the mystery of his purse. He was asleep almost as soon as he stretched himself between the crisp linen sheets.

***

It must be the wind in the tall pines. It must be the shuffle of the cows in the stable at milking time. Tom turned uneasily. The noise stopped, but now Tom was awake. He lay tense and scarcely breathing. Where was he?

It all came back to him quickly. He was no longer at home in the log cabin. He was no longer going to the stable to milk cows. He was in Williamsburg. He was supposed to be asleep in the home of his new master. There was the rustle again, and Tom realized it must be the long curtains of the big double bed being pulled closed carefully.

"So he thought he could sneak to bed without my hearing him. The thief." Tom's anger came hot and so violent that he hardly realized what he did. Slipping quickly from his low trundle, he took one step across the room and flung back the curtains of the bed. The night had cleared, and a full moon shone in the window, lighting up the white face that rose startled from the pillow.

"You low-down—you utter swine!" Tom's voice was muffled, choking with anger. "Where's my purse? You can insult me, call me a stinking backwoodsman, but you cannot rob me. What have you done with my money?"

"Money, purse?" James was half on his knees now. "I've not touched your money. How should I know you had money? Do you think I go snooping into the affairs of ignorant fools like you?"

This was too much. Tom hurled himself forward. Swinging with his right arm, he caught the other boy a fierce blow on the ear. There was a cry. Tom flung his great hand over James' mouth. With the other, he twisted the terrified boy's arm fiercely behind him. He hardly knew his own strength. James gasped and choked. There was a stifled moan as Tom removed his hand. The skinny body went limp. Great sobs welled out of the boy. Tom released the puny arm and staggered back.

Could this be? Was it true that the great bully, the great swaggerer was crying there with his head deep in the pillow? Tom stood a moment by the edge of the bed looking down on the figure which now without all its fine coats and frills appeared such a weakling compared to his own wild strength.

The only sound in the room were the sobs that seemed endless. Tom listened. What had he done? He must have been crazy or perhaps still half asleep to have done this thing. Finally he was able to speak. He came toward the bed again.

"I'm sorry," he said almost in a whisper. "I'm sorry for attacking you and for accusing you of stealing my purse. It is all I had in the world. It was my mother's and my little sister's too, and it is gone. I must have been half asleep."

There was no answer, but the sound of the crying was softer now. Tom waited. "You've not been very friendly." He felt suddenly that he should not do all the apologizing.

"I know." The head half turned. Even in the moonlight it was easy to see the great red tear stains on the pale cheeks. "Everybody hates me. Even Jake, the blacksmith you saw me with, hates me. He only gives me tips on the horses because he wants half of what I win. I'm—I'm—"

The boy turned, flung his head down, and was silent. Tom waited a long time. This was the most terrible thing that had ever happened to him. He couldn't move. He couldn't speak. Then slowly he stepped back. He put his hands on the red and white curtains. He closed them slowly, but as he did so the face turned once more. The moon fell on it like a strange spotlight. Was that, could it be that the boy was smiling? Whether it was a shy smile or one of those ugly sneers young James had made himself such a master of, Tom did not wait to find out. After yanking the curtains tightly shut, he sank into his tiny simple bed and fell instantly asleep.

CHAPTER 7

Tom woke early in the morning. As he was used only to the sound of the wind in the trees, the rattle of the carts and carriages and the thudding of the horses' hoofs on the street roused him. He lay still, listening. A long streak of warm sun played across his face.

Having no desire to face James again, Tom slipped quietly from his bed and pulled on his clothes. Opening the door as noiselessly as possible, he glided down the stairs and was soon standing in the back garden of the Purdie house.

The cold wind of the day before had gone down, and the sun shone warm and comforting from a blue-white sky. Tom stood a moment looking at the neat little garden, sprucely painted outbuildings, and, at the farthest end, what must be the stable. Mr. Purdie had given permission for Tom's dog to sleep with old John the coachman, and Tom was anxious to see how his little troublemaker had come through the night.

As he walked down the neat center path lined with a small box hedge, the sweet smell of cedar chips rose with the gray smoke from the brick building directly behind the house. "That must be the kitchen," thought Tom as he sniffed hungrily. "Smells like fresh bread." He smiled to himself. Next to the kitchen stood the small square smokehouse, and opposite that, the laundry and creamery. Tom couldn't resist poking his head in the door of the last. Brown earthenware jugs of fresh milk

stood in rows, and bowls of yellow butter shone golden in the
cool darkness.

The vegetable and flower gardens made Tom chuckle a bit
to himself as he saw how each was so neatly bounded by its
own little hedge. How different from the great wild-corn fields,
cut from the wilderness, that he had been used to plowing.
Reaching over a hedge, he plucked a sprig of sweet-smelling
lavender from the tiny herb garden, and crushing it in his rough
hands, he held it to his nose. It made him think once more
of his mother and the only luxury she ever allowed herself,
the dried lavender sprinkled in the chest where she kept her
treasured wedding dress and Milly's tiny baby clothes.

Tom pulled the stable door back. A great chestnut mare
neighed suspiciously. "Shh! I'll not harm you." Tom patted the
horse gently and pushed in beside her, rubbing her soft nose
affectionately. There came a little bark, a rustle in the clean
straw, and a tiny white head appeared.

"Well, if you didn't make yourself right at home." Tom
laughed as his little dog, her white fur spotted with bits of
yellow straw, began dancing and yipping about his legs.
Bending down, he picked her up gently. Then, brushing the fur
back from the little black button eyes, Tom whispered happily:
"You're all right. By gad, you look better than you did last night.
Old John must have fed you well. And he brushed you, too."

The white hair looked silky and clean, for the dried mud and
slush had been combed out and the fur neatly brushed all over
the little dog's back. Tom hugged her tightly.

"Oh, I hope I can keep you always. I've thought of a name for
you, too. You look like her with your black button eyes and your
hair always tumbling about your face. You look like the little
one, Milly. Yes, that's what I'll call you, Milly. And it will make it

easier to be away from home if I have a little Milly of my own to stay with me all the time."

The old feeling of loneliness came back. Tom squeezed the little dog until she squealed and, wiggling in his arms, jumped to the floor. Tom looked up. The grinning face of John the coachman was looking at him. The servant chuckled.

"Nice dog, suh." The old man spoke gently, as if in some strange way he had understood what Tom was thinking as he stood hugging his dog.

"Yes." Tom was embarrassed and could feel his face turning red. "Yes, I found her yesterday."

The old man stood brushing the hay and straw from his rumpled blue trousers. "William done told me the governor 'most run the little dog down, and you picked her up."

"I hope Mr. Purdie will let me keep her. Do you think so, John?" Tom spoke so eagerly that the old servant looked up in surprise. A huge grin spread over his face; he scratched at his crinkly white hair.

"Keep it? Why sure, boy, Mista Purdie wouldn't never take a dog away from nobody; he's just that kind. Don't you worry, boy, you'll keep your dog alright."

The morning was a long and bewildering one for Tom, for no sooner had he returned to the house and eaten his breakfast than Mr. Purdie took him into the small shop that he kept at the back of his house and began outfitting him with his new city clothes. Tom stood miserably, looking over the neatly arranged shelves, as Mr. Purdie fitted shirts, coats, and trousers to his new apprentice. There were rows of fine laces and Irish linens, rolls of heavy cloth, white and colored satins, and along one entire wall were bonnets and ladies' hats, which Mr.

Purdie assured him were of the latest fashion. Then there were beautiful red capes for ladies, some trimmed with ermine, and short capes of heavy wools and lighter materials.

"All from London, some even from Paris, all imported by me." Mr. Purdie beamed happily as he bustled about pulling boxes and packages down from shelves and holding up various sizes and colors to Tom.

"You're a big lad, Tom." He sighed at last. "But I think now I have an outfit that will make you a bit more respectable about the town. Nothing against your own clothes, of course. Fine for the woods and all that, but not quite what we wear here in Williamsburg."

With that he handed what looked to poor Tom like enough clothes to last his whole family for several years. There was a clean cotton shirt and stock for every day in the week. There were three pairs of dark green breeches, a waistcoat with gold braid down the front and brass buttons, a fine dark green coat, and a three-cornered hat to match. Last of all came four pairs of white cotton stockings and garters to hold them up.

"Now, boy, go upstairs and dress yourself." Mr. Purdie patted the bewildered Tom on the shoulder. "I'll be glad to see you dressed and ready for work."

Tom struggled for nearly an hour with his new clothes, but at last he looked approvingly in the mirror at the young man in stiff stock, white shirt, trim waistcoat, and neat-fitting coat. He placed his three-cornered hat jauntily on the side of his head, pulled his long white stockings tighter under his knee breeches, wiggled his poor toes in their new prisons of stiff black leather, and was ready to rejoin Mr. Purdie.

Mr. Purdie walked briskly as they started for the shop, and as he walked, he talked earnestly to Tom.

"Miss Peachy seems to feel as I do, Tom, that it is not too good an arrangement for you and James to share his room." The old man hesitated. Tom looked quickly up at him.

Could it be that Miss Peachy had told her husband about the purse? No, Tom decided that was impossible.

"We were wondering last evening what we should provide for you," Mr. Purdie continued, "when I suddenly remembered the little attic room over the shop. There is a stove to keep you warm, and with a bit of fixing up and a little furniture from our house, you should be most comfortable there." Mr. Purdie looked at Tom. "You would not mind such an arrangement, boy?"

Mind! Tom was delighted. A room all of his own. A room where he could be quite independent to come and go as he pleased, the way he had always been used to doing. And best and most important of all, a room where he did not have to be constantly checking his feelings about James.

"Oh, that would be splendid, sir," he said eagerly. Then he hesitated. "Then could I—perhaps it would be all right for me to keep Milly?"

"Milly?" Mr. Purdie looked puzzled.

"Oh, I'm sorry, sir," Tom apologized, "that's what I've decided to call the dog. It's the name of my baby sister, and there's something about that little dog that reminds me of her."

Mr. Purdie smiled. Then his face became serious. "Well, I don't know. I don't really like the idea of a dog in the shop."

Tom's heart sank. "But—but, sir, I promise she'll be no trouble. She might even, sir—well, she might be sort of a watchdog."

At this suggestion Mr. Purdie threw back his head and gave a great, hearty laugh. "A watchdog, indeed, boy. Why I doubt if that little creature would scare a mouse. But—well, all right. I suppose you can keep her there if you like. But mind, she's not to get in the ink or the lampblack or the clean sheets of paper and she's not to be underfoot."

Tom smiled to himself as he remembered old John's words about Mr. Purdie's kindness.

"Oh, no, sir," he promised eagerly. "I swear she will never be a trouble."

CHAPTER 8

Tom was getting used to Williamsburg, and it seemed as if Williamsburg too were getting used to the ways of the young frontiersman. After two months Tom was now able to wear his stiff shoes without stumbling. He wore his white stock without feeling he was choking to death, and he was even willing to admit that having his hair close-cropped, instead of halfway to his shoulders, was considerably more handy when he was deep in black printer's ink all day long.

As for the good people of Williamsburg, they no longer stared after the rough-looking boy as he delivered their Gazette every Friday. Indeed, they found Tom's quick wit, sharpened by the ready give-and-take of hardy frontiersmen, a joy in the midst of the turned phrases and fine speeches they were accustomed to. Most everyone had a friendly greeting for Tom now as he, with little Milly trotting happily beside him, went up and down the Duke of Gloucester Street, round about the side streets, and even rode out to nearby plantations delivering Mr. Purdie's new paper.

So far the new sheet had done well. The subscribers seemed pleased, and the number of stops Tom had to make each week was growing all the time. In fact, Mr. Purdie wondered if Tom himself did not have something to do with this increasing popularity, for there was never an article of importance that the new apprentice did not read eagerly. He followed the troubles brewing up north in the hard-pressed Massachusetts Colony as eagerly as he read the letters from England telling of the outrageous behavior of the king and his provoking prime minister, Lord North. Mr. Purdie was not unaware of the fact that his new helper talked politics with anyone who would give him the time, and when an argument would grow heated, Mr. Purdie had heard young Tom challenge his opponent with, "But you must not have read the last article in Mr. Purdie's Gazette." Mr. Purdie knew then that his paper was due for a sale. Such a challenge could not be ignored.

Tom himself was happy. He liked the new life and was excited by all that went on about him. He liked his new friends and the opportunity to argue with his contemporaries and listen eagerly to his elders as they discussed the politics of the day in the shop. As to his work, that was the only disappointment Tom felt. With the great effort of getting out the new paper, there had been little time left for Mr. Purdie to teach what Tom had come so far to learn: the printer's trade. He had picked up what he could by watching his master, but there were many things that he wished the older man had more time to explain to him and that he had more time to practice by himself. It seemed to him sometimes that he would never master this craft, for even in so little a thing as mixing the ink, he still performed like an amateur, much to the amusement of Mr. Purdie.

"Tom, Tom, boy, take it easy," he would say, peering over his tiny spectacles as he roosted on his high stool above the type cases. "By gad, you're a real printer's devil. You can't help a sneeze or two when you're mixing the ink. Here, let me show you once more." The little man slipped off the stool and crossed the room. Tom sneezed again, and every time he sneezed, the lampblack flew into the air in a feathery black cloud. It blew into Tom's eyes and went up his nose, which only caused him to sneeze again even harder than before.

Mr. Purdie grinned. "Look, just a little lampblack at a time. Then pour the varnish on gently. Use a slow, easy roll to mix it. Don't go at it as if you were chopping down one of those big trees way out there in Frederick County." Mr. Purdie's eyes twinkled behind the little spectacles. "Slowly, slowly. See, it goes in smooth as silk."

Tom grinned in spite of himself. His white teeth glistened in his black face. He tried again, following the slow motions of Mr. Purdie, and gradually the lampblack clung to the varnish, and the ink began to look like thick black molasses. Then he added the whale oil to make it pour more easily into the great earthenware jug that always stood handy by the presses.

Mr. Purdie nodded approval. "You're getting the hang of it, boy. Don't be discouraged. Mr. Benjamin Franklin did not learn overnight to be the greatest printer in the colonies. Come, I'll test you a bit with the type."

This was the chance Tom had been waiting for. He spent every free moment trying to learn the type cases and the location of each letter. Mr. Purdie had pinned at the top of his type case a chart of where each letter was kept, and Tom, holding the composing stick firmly in his left hand, had worked hard to set up articles that might be used in the Gazette. For the Gazette was Tom's greatest ambition. He knew as soon as he hung the first edition up to dry that to be allowed to set real articles for the Gazette and to be trusted to print an edition alone was his true ambition. He would never feel he had attained what he had come so far to learn until Mr. Purdie permitted him to set type for the Gazette. But now, in the rare moment when the older man stood over him to watch him pick the letters as he called them from the type cases, Tom nervously confused the letters p and q.

Mr. Purdie chuckled good-naturedly. "Mind your p's and q's, boy. That's the first rule of printing. But that's enough for today. I have this announcement, for the opening of Dr. Galt's and Dr. Pasteur's new apothecary shop, that must be run through the press. The post rider will be here very soon, and you know what a hubbub the shop will be then."

Tom liked the work at the press and felt that, at least here, he was beginning to master his new trade. Pouring a thin stream of the black ink he had just mixed from its earthenware jug, he covered the heavy stone that stood beside the press. Then, taking the great leather-covered ink ball, he turned it slowly in the ink and carefully inked the announcement Mr. Purdie had set up. He had learned the hard way that too much ink made great black blots, and too little made an impression that was too faint to read. Placing a clean sheet of paper in position, he laid his hands on the long wooden handle of the press.

"Now, slow and even." Mr. Purdie watched critically from the front of the shop. Tom pulled. "There, now, a bit harder at the end." Tom leaned back, bracing his feet. "Now, back again."

Tom swung the big handle back into place. The plates rose slowly. The carriage slid back, and Tom looked eagerly at the impression he had just pulled. He handed it to Mr. Purdie.

"Very nice, Tom." The older man looked pleased as he examined the small white sheet glistening with fresh ink. "That's a clean, clear job. If you'd twisted that 'devil's tail' any harder, the letters would have shown through; any lighter would not have been as easy to read."

Tom chuckled as he always did when Mr. Purdie referred to the long wooden handle of the press as "the devil's tail." There were many phrases and turns of speech to do with the press that had amused Tom, but of them all, he felt that "to twist the devil's tail" was the one which he liked the best.

Tom worked hard for the rest of the morning, and he enjoyed the rhythm and satisfaction of the work. He liked the creak of the press and the smell of the fresh ink.

It wasn't until about noon that there came the clatter of hoofs in the street outside. The huge gray horse of the post rider reared as its wiry master pulled rein before the printing office. Mr. Purdie hurried out, took the two bulging leather sacks handed down to him, and exchanged a short greeting with the young rider as the great horse stood breathing heavily for a moment.

Hardly had the two disappeared around the turn by the Capitol building, which stood at the end of the Duke of Gloucester Street, than the printing office was filled with eager, curious townsfolk—some watching hopefully for a letter directed to them, some waiting news of the rest of the world, and some on hand merely to exchange the gossip of the day with their neighbors. There were small packages of books, fresh letter paper, and music sheets Mr. Purdie had ordered sent down from Philadelphia. Then the letters from the other colonies were opened. The gazettes and newspapers from up north were unfolded, and it was no time at all before the political argument of the day had begun.

Tom listened eagerly above the creak of the press as the talk grew heated and tempers grew short over the most disputed topic of the day: the forthcoming Virginia Convention, which was to be held in a few weeks up in Richmond.

"The arrogance of our governor, daring to allow an armed ship, a man-of-war, right here in our own York River." A young man addressed as Mr. Saunders took a long clay pipe from his mouth and spoke with feeling. "It's certainly not hard for even the most ignorant to see that things are not going to get any better between us and the mother country with such arrogance flouted in our faces."

An older man, whom Tom did not recognize, had sat tense and quiet during most of the talk. He spoke thoughtfully now. "Eh, to think that we have had to move our meeting of the Virginia Convention up to Richmond because we are afraid of what our own governor might do to us. That's a bad sign, indeed."

At this there was a stir in one corner of the shop. An old man, so stooped and wrinkled that he gave the impression of no life or blood at all in his tiny face, spoke, his voice shaking with anger.

"What's this?" his voice cracked. "What's all this talk of a British governor attacking his own colony? Pshaw! What are we coming to, I ask you? It's nonsense, sheer nonsense, I tell you, all this business of not buying British goods, spinning and weaving here at home so as not to trade with our mother country. Sending food and provisions to that stiff-necked colony of Massachusetts. By gad, they ought to be thankful the king did not hang them all for their behavior. Rebels, all of them, a pack of worthless rebels. If the king and Parliament have no right to tax them, then pray, who has? He should have done worse than just sealing up their harbor."

There was a hushed silence in the shop. Tom let his hands lie limp on the big wooden handle. Nobody spoke, and the old man continued. "I tell you, we're Virginians. What does it matter to us if the harbor of Boston is closed tight as a drum? That's not our concern. If we take up their quarrel, we're apt to have war. War, I tell you!" He fairly shrieked out the words.

Tom looked from one to the other of the men gathered about the front of the office. Mr. Purdie, still holding the article he had been reading, rose from his desk and came forward. He spoke quietly, choosing his words carefully.

"Eh, we might start a war, and nobody knows it better than we loyal Virginians, Mr. Jones, but there's worse things than war perhaps. If the British government can send ships to bottle up the harbor of Boston, what's to stop it from doing the same to us? Already a man-of-war lies in the York River. There may be troops aboard her, and if soldiers can be quartered on the people of Boston, what's to stop them from being quartered on us, too?"

"Good, Mr. Purdie." Dr. Galt spoke with authority.

"Eh." The young Mr. Saunders, who had first brought on the discussion, spoke angrily. "I ask you, Mr. Jones—" he addressed the old man who now stood defiantly in the middle of the group, "I ask you, sir, when must a man stand up and say, 'I will be free. Free to govern myself. Free to tax myself. Free to speak out and say what I think.' There's no use giving in to His Majesty anymore, nor his rotten Lord North and that fawning Parliament of his. We've been petitioning them for ten years to let us have more representation if we are to be taxed by the king. Ever since the first Stamp Tax was imposed, we've been sending petitions and pleas. Not even Mr. Benjamin Franklin has been able to win a point for us. By gad, it's time we showed that as true Englishmen, we are ready to stand up and speak for ourselves, even if it does mean the bloody state of war."

"Pshaw!" Old Mr. Jones raised a thin, shaking fist in the air. "You're rebels, revolutionaries, I say, every mother's son of you, and you should hang for this treasonous talk." The words were fairly spat at the group, and the slamming door rattled the glass in its moldings as the old man stamped angrily from the printing office.

Mr. Saunders took a step forward, his face white with anger. Dr. Galt laid a steady hand on his shoulder. "Never mind, Saunders. Old Jones has always been against us. We mustn't let him anger us. He's too old to matter much now."

"Yes, but it's the narrowness of his ideas that angers me. Can't he see that it's now or never? Either we stand up now against this intolerant treatment of the king, or we are lost. By gad"— young Mr. Saunder's rage increased as he talked—"by gad, if Mr. Patrick Henry doesn't win the vote up in Richmond next week to have our militia armed and trained properly, we're lost. It's troops, muskets, and men we need now. That's the only way left to us to speak to His Majesty if he should try to bring British soldiers into our colony in order to force his demands on us. Troops, troops, and more troops, that's what we must have."

Tom laid his hands back on the handle of the press and resumed his work once more. He watched the little group break up and did not miss the look of anxious worry on Mr. Purdie's face as he went back to his desk.

CHAPTER 9

It was late when Tom completed the announcements for Dr. Galt and Dr. Pasteur's apothecary shop. Mr. Purdie had already left the office when the final copy was laid out to dry.

After taking Milly for a short walk, as he always did when he had finished his work, Tom wearily blew out the candles in the big chandelier and climbed the steep stairs to his little room above the shop. Miss Peachy had gone to much trouble to make it comfortable for him. When Tom assured her he was not used to so soft a mattress, such a pile of fine blankets, and fresh curtains at his windows, she only smiled and said not to keep bothering her.

Lighting a small fire in his little iron stove, for the early March night had a nip to it, Tom sat at his pine desk and wrote a long letter to his mother. The pen scratched in the silence as Tom told of the daily routine of his life during the past fortnight. He seldom let more than that time pass without a letter to his ma or his old teacher, Mr. Thruston. To the latter he wrote eagerly of the political talk in the shop, of the important men, such as Mr. Washington or Patrick Henry, whom he had seen or had news of. He knew Mr. Thruston was anxious to keep up with all that was happening in the capital as well as to learn all he could of the troubles up north. To his mother Tom wrote of the good food Miss Peachy fed him, for he ate his evening meal with the Purdie family, fixing his meager

breakfast in his own room and eating the fresh bread and
cheese Mr. Purdie brought to the shop at noon. He told of the
funny remarks of Alex and William, Mr. Purdie's two youngest
sons, and of the foolish pranks they were constantly playing on
the household. But of James he said little or nothing. Indeed,
there was little to say, for he scarcely saw the young dandy, who
seemed to dine and wine anywhere but at home. As to Tom's
purse, it was never referred to again between them, and after
Miss Peachy had made certain inquiries, there seemed little else
that could be done, and Tom was forced to accept the bitter loss
as best he could.

The candle flickered in the little tin candlestick. Tom's head
dropped forward on the desk. He was not asleep, yet not really
awake, but too tired to continue his writing. As he sat there,
his head slouched forward, he thought of the two months that
had passed—of how much he had had to learn and how hard
some of it had been. For the first time in many weeks, he was
homesick again. He clenched his great strong fists. If he could
see his ma only for a day… And he would like to see how the
corn was coming in the west field he'd plowed before he left. It
was early to plow it and hard work, too, but he knew he must
if Old Man Thompson were to plant it for his ma when the
warm weather came. Had there been a little new heifer as they'd
hoped? Tom saw the cabin standing strong, rough, and secure
under the great pines. And little Milly—Tom wondered how she
was. Had she grown in two months? What words could she say
now? She had only started to try when he left.

Tom rose from the desk, wiping his eyes with his ink-stained
fingers, then stopped. The ink made him think. He had
forgotten an important job in the shop. He had hung the ink
ball back in place without cleaning it as Mr. Purdie had given
him strict orders to do each night. An uncleaned ink ball

became stiff and hard and would not spread the ink properly.

Starting toward the door, Tom looked down at the white bundle of fur curled happily at the bottom of the bed. Milly stirred and opened her black button eyes as Tom brushed the long hair back from them gently.

"I'm so glad I found you, Milly," he half whispered, slouching for a moment on the bed beside her. "It would have been mighty hard to be all alone up here if I had not been allowed to keep you."

Tom knew no more after that. His eyes closed. He stretched himself on the bed and slept.

Then he stirred, shivering a little. He put out his hand and felt something furry and warm. It was dark in the room now. The candle had burned itself out.

"Milly." Tom smiled to himself in the darkness. "You little devil. Get back to the end of the bed. How dare you come crawling and growling up here to my end?"

Tom put out his hand again to push the little dog back where she belonged, when suddenly he stopped. There was something strange in the dog's manner. Why was she growling so softly as if speaking to him? Why had she awakened him? Tom lay very still and listened.

Could that be a noise in the shop down below? No, that was not possible. But yes, there it was again—the soft, faint sound of a chair pushed or perhaps bumped by mistake in the darkness. Tom rubbed his hand over his face. He must be dreaming. Half sitting up and placing his hand over Milly's mouth to be sure she did not bark, Tom listened intently.

Just then there came the unmistakable sound of a drawer

being opened. The post office money! Tom knew in a second where Mr. Purdie kept all the money he took in or had to pay out for the post office.

Tom's thoughts were quite clear now. There was no longer any doubt in his mind. Somebody was in the office below, and anybody coming at this hour meant no good to Mr. Purdie. Sliding his feet off the bed, Tom stood up. His early training, creeping through the woods as he searched for rabbits and partridge made it easy for him to move now without any sound at all. He made his way to the head of the narrow stairs leading down to the office. He stood listening. There was no mistaking the sound again. Somebody was pulling open the money drawer.

Tom's stockinged feet sought each step without the creaking of a single board. He was quickly in the back of the office. The weak flicker of the street lamp outside threw a tiny beam of light through the big windows at the front of the shop. Silhouetted against this was the figure of a man stooping over the open money drawer of the post office.

Tom did not hesitate. He threw himself headlong down the little steps to the front of the shop. As he passed the press on which he had so recently been working, he grabbed for the uncleaned ink ball.

The man straightened. Tom was upon him. Waving the ink ball in the air, he brought it down with a crash on the intruder's head. The man staggered, then recovered. Before Tom could regain his balance to defend himself, there came a stinging blow in his face. For a moment he went blind. The flickering light from the street lamp went out. There was a terrible roar in Tom's head. He sagged forward, caught himself on Mr. Purdie's high stool, and balanced for a moment. There was a frantic barking, a wild curse, and the sound of a struggle.

Tom's head cleared. Lifting himself up on the stool, he clung to the type cases and looked over. The robber was half out of the window. Attached to one of his legs was a small white object clinging fiercely as the leg went up and down. The man was caught. He could go neither forward nor back. There he lay, half in and half out of the window, cursing horribly.

Tom steadied himself, took a hard grip on the ink ball, and throwing back the bolt on the front door, rushed out and began beating the helpless man unmercifully about the head and ears, while calling for help as loud as he could.

"Stop, thief! Stop! Stop! Mr. Purdie, Mr. Purdie!"

There was a quick thudding of feet. Questioning calls in the night. A shout to answer Tom's "Stop, thief!" And within what seemed to Tom hardly more than a few seconds, a crowd of men and boys gathered from nowhere.

The burglar was quickly pulled from the shop window. His hands were bound behind him. He stood there angry, cursing, and black as the night that surrounded him, for the uncleaned ink ball still had enough ink left on it to cover his face completely. Tom doubted if even the man's best friend would have recognized him now.

"But, Tom—" Tom heard Mr. Purdie behind him puffing and wheezing. "Tom, boy." Mr. Purdie was patting him on the back now, grasping him by the hand and fairly dancing about, looking quite ridiculous with his bald head shining in the lamplight, for he had not stopped to put on his wig. His fat legs showed naked from his nightshirt and jacket that he had hurriedly thrown over himself. "Tom, you're a brave fellow indeed. And how lucky that the ink ball, against all my instructions, had never been cleaned tonight." Mr. Purdie broke into a happy chuckle.

CHAPTER 10

Tom had an invitation to breakfast the next morning, as each member of the Purdie family felt it was their special privilege to quiz the young hero about the events of the night before. Even old Betty had to find an excuse to come all the way in from the kitchen house to hear the tale straight from the mouth of young "Mista Tom." Alex and William sat with their mouths open. Ever since the first night they saw Tom, in his rough leather jacket and coonskin cap, he had been their secret hero, and here was a deed worthy of anyone's dreams. Tom told and retold the story, giving all the credit to Milly, of course, for after all, if it hadn't been for her waking Tom and then catching the man by the heels, he surely would have escaped long before Tom recovered himself. Mr. Purdie sat at the head of the table, purring and chuckling and nodding Tom's way with approval as he modestly tried to explain that he had had little to do with the actual capture.

There was only one person who finished his waffles as quickly as possible and left the room without a single question. James seemed to dislike the entire event. He looked paler than ever this morning, and Tom thought once, when he surprised James looking at him, that there was the same sickly half grin, half sneer that had flitted across the face on the pillow that first night in Williamsburg. Mr. Purdie noticed James' reaction, too, for when he addressed him, asking if he were not glad that Tom had saved what would have been a large sum of money for Mr.

Purdie to lose, James merely grunted approval. It was almost as if it were more than he could stand to see his father so delighted with his apprentice.

"This is all very well," said Mr. Purdie, pushing back his chair at last. "All this hero worship, my boy, but this morning I'm afraid we have some rather unpleasant work to do. It's up to us to go over to the jail and identify that man as the one who entered the office."

Tom did not relish this idea at all. It was one thing to catch a man in the act of stealing your employer's money, but another to be the one responsible for having that same man sentenced to what Tom knew all too well would be a very severe punishment if not death itself.

The jail was located over behind the Capitol and was a small squat building of red brick. The stock and pillory were at one side. Here a wretched, dirty woman stood screaming and making ugly remarks at the passersby, while a thin little, half-starved man sat silently brooding in the stocks beside her. Tom felt sorry for them both, but Mr. Purdie made some comment about their being nuisances to the town, which Tom did not understand.

Once inside the jail, Tom immediately wished he were out again, for the very smell of the place made him feel sick. Mr. Peter Pelham, the jailer, welcomed them in the hallway and led the way to a small waiting room beyond. Tom stood first on one foot, then on the other, looking about at the rough wooden furniture, listening to the sad crackling of the undernourished fire, and wishing more than he had ever wished anything in his whole life that he weren't mixed up in this business.

Mr. Pelham, a thin little man, cackled and chatted with Mr. Purdie until Tom thought he couldn't stand the suspense any longer. He must see the man he had been so instrumental in sending to jail. Who was he? Was he some tramp who had wandered into the capital? Was he somebody Tom would recognize? But Mr. Pelham was in high spirits and, rubbing his long, pointed fingers together, he cracked the knuckles incessantly and seemed quite unaware of Tom's anxieties. Tom examined him closely, although he knew him already by sight, for Mr. Pelham, as well as being the jailer, was the organist at Bruton Parish Church where Tom went each Sunday with the Purdies.

This extraordinarily versatile man also gave spinet and harpsichord lessons to the wealthy young ladies of the town. On nights when there was a theatrical performance to be seen, Mr. Pelham was always on hand to furnish music for the evening. By these greatly varied means he was able to make a respectable living for himself, which would not have been the case if he had stuck only to his jail.

"Well," Mr. Pelham's high voice grated on Tom's anxious ears, "I've washed and scrubbed your man for you." He smiled an eager little smile. "You did a good job on him, Tom, all right. Why he was so covered with black, it took most of a whole bar of soap to get off even the first layer." The high, cackling laugh rasped out again, and Tom winced. "But come, we'll fetch him in and find out who he is and what he was up to last night."

Tom did not wish to accompany Mr. Pelham and Mr. Purdie further into the jail, but he was motioned forward by the jailer, and there was no way to avoid it. Going down a short flight of steps, they passed along a narrow corridor with heavily locked and chained doors stretching the length of it. Through the iron bars that covered the small window in each door, thin pleading hands stretched forward as Mr. Pelham walked by. Desperate, sad, and angry voices pleaded with the jailer to listen to them;

to fetch them food, or to carry a note to a relation who would immediately come to their relief. Mr. Pelham paid no attention whatever to these interruptions but walked quickly to the last door. Turning a huge iron key in the lock and sliding a great bolt and chain, he opened the door slowly.

Inside this room it was almost dark. The only light came from a small window at one end. At first Tom could make out only dim black forms, but gradually his eyes grew accustomed to the darkness, and he saw that the room contained at least eight or ten men. Some sat leaning against the walls. Some lay on the floor, which was half covered with dirty straw, and in the farthest corner was a single bed. On this lay a solitary figure stretched at full length.

"Mr. Purdie wishes to see you. Here, you, who tried to rob Mr. Purdie last night. Come here." Mr. Pelham's voice broke into an angry squeak as no figure in the room made the least effort to move. With a quick fidgety step, the jailer hurried across the room and poked the figure on the cot. "You, you scoundrel. Do as I tell you. Come here. Follow me at once."

With that, he gave the prisoner a sharp rap on the head with his iron key. The man started up angrily. Even in the dim light Tom could see that he wore irons on both hands, and as he swung his legs over the side of the cot, there was a sound of heavy chains rattling together.

A sudden ray of strong sun slanted through the window and fell directly on the face of the prisoner. Tom gasped.

"No, no—not you."

"What, what is it, Tom?" Mr. Purdie took his arm. "Do you know this man? Who is he, Tom?"

Tom looked again at the face he had not been able to

recognize through the heavy coating of ink the night before. There was no mistaking Mr. Valentine!

Mr. Valentine returned Tom's stare without a flicker of so much as an eyelid. "Surely," thought Tom, his mind in a wild turmoil of confusion, "surely he must know me. He must remember that we have met and when." But there was nothing on the other man's face to indicate that he had ever seen young Tom Cartwright before.

"We've had a bit of a chat," Mr. Pelham began when they returned to the waiting room at the front of the jail, bringing the prisoner clanking along behind them. "I've looked him over pretty carefully. Nothing concealed, nothing you'd miss from the shop, Mr. Purdie, nothing but an old purse with two shillings in it. He says it's his."

"A purse!" Tom could have bitten off his tongue the moment these words slipped from his mouth.

"Eh, a purse." Mr. Pelham looked at Tom curiously. "Here it is, boy."

The jailer reached into the deep pocket of his coat and laid a crumpled, worn leather purse on the table. It was Tom's. There was no mistaking the way his mother had stitched it for him. There was no mistaking the small metal clasp with which she had fastened it. There were not two purses like that in the whole of Virginia.

Tom felt the three men looking at him. He knew his cheeks had flushed crimson. He could feel his hands shake.

"Why, Tom—" Mr. Purdie moved to his side quickly. "Tom, tell me, what's the matter? You're not sick? The excitement of last night isn't just telling on you, is it, boy?"

Tom could not answer. He knew too well what terrible punishment would be given the man standing shackled and silent on the other side of the table if it became known that this purse had been stolen from Tom. For stealing the purse, he would be branded in the hand as a thief, but for the stealing of the purse and the attempted robbery, the punishment would unquestionably be hanging. How could Tom ever live with himself again if he knew he were responsible for sending a man to the gallows?

"Nothing," he said. "It's nothing, Mr. Purdie." Tom's eyes sought those of the prisoner waiting—waiting for Tom's answer. As he heard the boy's words, Mr. Valentine's head snapped up. Clear, straight, and eager, his eyes sought Tom's.

"But you know this man?" Mr. Purdie pressed him further.

"Yes," Tom answered cautiously. He could see Mr. Valentine watching him closely, waiting to hear what he would say. "Yes," Tom proceeded. "I have seen him once before. He befriended me on my first night in Williamsburg, showing me the way to Mr. Purdie's. Indeed, he went out of his way to take me to the printing office."

Mr. Purdie and Mr. Pelham listened intently. A look of bewildering surprise showed on both their faces. They turned toward the prisoner questioningly.

"You befriended this boy once?" asked Mr. Purdie.

"Yes, if you wish to call it that. I merely showed him your shop." The thin lips curled into the queer, crooked smile that Tom remembered so well.

"Perhaps, then, perhaps you're not too bad a fellow after all, despite your actions last night. What you've said will be in his favor, Tom."

"Eh, may even have saved his skinny neck from the noose." Mr. Pelham's ill-timed wit was almost more than Tom could stand at that moment.

"Now if only they don't ask more about the purse. If only they forget about that," Tom thought over and over, and perhaps he willed it so hard that he forced the others to do as he wished for no further mention was made of it before the prisoner was led away to his cell once more.

CHAPTER 11

When the terrible interview at the jail was over, Tom had but one thought. He must get to Miss Peachy as soon as possible in order to tell her of the finding of his purse. He must bind her to the secret that Tom knew now must never be told, for he had gone too far in this whole ugly business to be able to retrace his steps again.

After dinner that night, although so tired he could hardly eat even the special pecan pie Old Betty had made for him, Tom did not go back to his own room immediately, as was his habit. Instead, he sat about with the family waiting, hoping that Mr. Purdie and James, who for some reason had eaten at home that night, might leave the room or retire early. James noticed how Tom sat and talked with his father, and at last could not resist a sarcastic comment on the matter.

"Well, Tom," he sneered as he lolled back in his chair, looking at Tom with the little slit eyes Tom had grown to hate and distrust so completely. "So our hero is not as anxious to return to his own quarters tonight as usual. Not quite as brave as last night perhaps."

Tom said nothing, and James continued his little act until at last Mr. Purdie became irritated and ordered his son either to speak civilly or not at all. At this, James stamped out of the room in a huff, his face and ears flushed with anger at the public reprimand. Mr. Purdie grunted in disgust as James slammed the front door, then, knocking the ashes from his pipe, he went off to the stable to see about the chestnut mare, which had gone lame that afternoon.

This was the opportunity Tom had been waiting for. He looked at Miss Peachy sitting there seemingly occupied with her embroidery. She wore a soft dress of deep blue, and her skirts fell about her in graceful folds, making her look almost regal as her little fingers moved with great skill on the screen she was making. Tom could not find the right words to begin, but somehow Miss Peachy knew he had something to say to her. Looking up, she smiled.

"It has all been hard for you, Tom," she said gently. "I was sorry Mr. Purdie felt you must go to the jail. It is one thing to want justice done, but another one to be the one to cause the death or suffering that will no doubt be the punishment of this man."

"That's it, Miss Peachy," Tom blurted out. "That's what I wanted to tell you. Of course, there's no way to save the man,

because he did try to rob Mr. Purdie. But did you know that"—
he hesitated a moment, then continued—"that my purse was
found on him?"

The sewing dropped from Miss Peachy's hands. "Tom," she
gasped. "Tom, no. How could this be?"

Tom heard not only the surprise, but he thought he
recognized relief, too, in Miss Peachy's voice. She had
never mentioned the name of James in connection with the
disappearance of the purse, but Tom knew her fears, for he had
seen her searching James' room when he first told her his purse
was gone.

"Thank heavens, we never told Mr. Purdie," Miss Peachy
almost whispered. "Now he will never know . . ." The words
trailed off, and Tom wondered what they might have been.

"I did not tell them it was mine when I saw it today. Was that
wrong, Miss Peachy?" Tom gulped and looked into the gentle
face for help.

There was a long silence. Tom was afraid. Would she make
him tell about the robbery of his purse now that there was no
reason to suspect a member of her own family?

"Once," he continued pleadingly, "I saw a man's hand they
had branded for stealing." Tom clenched his own strong hands
nervously. "It was red and purple around the letters. The man
could never again in all his life hide the fact that he had once
stolen a lady's purse at a fair. He was branded a thief for as long
as he lived. People would never believe him again, no matter
how straight and honestly he might live after that."

Miss Peachy, getting up, walked slowly toward Tom. She
laid her hand on his trembling shoulders. "No, Tom," she
said quietly. "No, the man will probably get severe enough

punishment without mention of the purse."

"Well!" Mr. Purdie flung open the door. "What's this, Peachy, the boy afraid? Come, Tom, lightning never strikes twice in the same place. It's late for you. Shall I walk as far as the shop?"

Tom could feel Miss Peachy stiffen as she stood beside him. For the first time since he had come to the house, he thought she spoke severely to her husband.

"Indeed, the boy's not afraid, Alexander. Quite the contrary, he's far braver than you have any notion of."

With that she said goodnight and hurried up the stairs. Mr. Purdie turned, puzzled, looking at Tom. "Now what could have got into the good woman? What's in the wind, Tom, boy? I've not said anything to hurt you?"

"No, sir," Tom said slowly. "No, nothing at all, sir. It's just"— he smiled—"well, I guess it's just that Miss Peachy, perhaps, thinks I'm more of a hero than I am."

Mr. Purdie clapped him on the back, and with a hearty laugh sent Tom off into the warm spring night.

CHAPTER 12

Mr. Patrick Henry was a fiery man. There were few who would deny that. To be sure, there were those who still tried to dismiss the rough, young lawyer from the mountain country as a firebrand and a rabble rouser, but there was no denying that he had courage. He had never feared to say what he thought, and his words were becoming increasingly popular.

When he first took his seat in the House of Burgesses, he was the only member to speak out against the stamp tax. And when he finished, he had the courage to challenge the House: "If this be treason, then make the most of it."

Mr. Henry had a way of speaking and a way of using his voice that were rare, and he carried a power when he spoke that was moving both to behold and to listen to. He had gone as a delegate to the First Continental Congress in Philadelphia, in the fall of 1774, along with the Colonel George Washington, Mr. Peyton Randolph, and the others. Here the colonists met together for the first time in an effort to unite against what they termed taxation by the king without representation in his government. Mr. Henry had spoken brilliantly at Philadelphia, reminding the delegates that it was the British oppression itself that was doing away with the many boundaries that had heretofore separated the colonies.

Now in March of the year 1775, not yet six months since that first Congress in Philadelphia, it was rumored that Mr. Henry would make another great speech at the Virginia Convention being held in St. John's Church in Richmond. The biggest issue to be faced at the convention was whether or not the time had come for the Virginia militia to be assembled and trained. Discussions ran high and heated on this subject. There were those, like old Mr. Jones, who felt this was sheer treason, and there were others who felt that a resort to arms was the only road left open to the colonists now. Boston Harbor had been sealed up tight as a drum for almost a year, with British warships intercepting any attempts at trade outside the colony. If this was the punishment Boston received for hurling a few boxes of tea overboard in protest against unjust taxation, then there was no telling what might happen elsewhere.

Spring came with the daffodils bowing yellow and white behind every fence and hedge. The palace green was the color of emeralds, and the trees that lined the Duke of Gloucester Street were feathery with sticky new leaves.

The convention dragged on. Would the issue of the militia never be decided? Men and women alike craved an answer. Would the young men of Williamsburg be put into uniform and be trained to defend Virginia's rights against the aggressions of the king?

These were difficult times in the printing office, too. Mr. Purdie was to be the official printer for the convention, and the shop was a gathering place from morning to night. It was almost impossible to get any work done, and the publishing of the Gazette became increasingly difficult with Mr. Purdie and Tom working late into the night, when at last the arguments, gossip, and rumors were finished for the day. But now they waited anxiously for the final news from Richmond. It must be handled as quickly as possible, and each day of waiting made Mr. Purdie more impatient and nervous.

Not until the last day of the month did the final news reach Williamsburg. It came with the clatter of hoofbeats. It came with the young post rider sagging in the saddle from fatigue as he drew reign outside the shop.

"From the convention," the rider said in short, tired tones as Mr. Purdie reached for the portfolio. "To be printed as quickly as possible." The man gave his instructions to Mr. Purdie, who nodded hurriedly, as if anxious to be about the task on the instant.

The arrival of this white-flecked, tired horse with his weary young rider was like a signal flying mysteriously through the town. From the Raleigh Tavern, the King's Arms, from Mr. Chowning's, from the barbershop, the silversmith's, and the boot-maker's came the men. From the houses, the side streets, and from the market square came the women and children, eager, clamoring, questioning.

"What does it say, Mr. Purdie? Read it. Read us what they said at the convention."

Tom stood close to Mr. Purdie. His master's hands shook, his fingers scarcely able to open the fasteners. Then he glanced quickly at the contents in the hushed silence.

"Will they arm us? Is the story correct that they will make soldiers of us? What did Mr. Henry have to say?"

The questions came fast. Mr. Purdie was reading the long, handwritten sheets. He held up his hand for silence.

"Eh," he said slowly, "eh, you're to be soldiers. You're to arm, and the militia will be trained, horse troops and foot troops. It even says here what you're to carry as arms. You must have a good horse and a saddle and bridle if you're to belong to the horse troop. You must be armed with pistols and holster, a carbine or other short firelock, a cutting sword or a tomahawk. You must train your horse to stand the discharge of firearms and become acquainted with the exercise for cavalry."

He hesitated for a moment before reading further.

"What else? What else did they do up there in Richmond?" A voice spoke from the crowd, sounding impatient and eager. But others were turning away now. They had learned the answer to the question that had been on every mind since the delegates first went to Richmond. They began to scatter once more to the Raleigh, to the King's Arms, to Mr. Chowning's, and to the market square. They returned to the barber, the silversmith's, to the boot-maker's, and to their houses. They drifted slowly, the husbands, the fathers, and the sons who knew now that they would soon be called to carry arms and perhaps even fight against their mother country, to fight for their rights—for their freedom.

Only a few followed Mr. Purdie and Tom back into the shop.

"Quick, Tom, set up this notice for the Gazette." Mr. Purdie stood at his desk. His quill pen scratched on the rough paper. Tom read the announcement as it was handed to him.

"The printer begs leave to inform the gentlemen of the late

convention that he only received some part of their proceedings late last night and the remainder this day at one o'clock." Mr. Purdie promised to use all haste in getting the proceedings on the press and distributed.

As he sat on his high stool, slowly, carefully setting the announcement, Tom listened eagerly to the talk of the men at the front of the office.

"Eh, Mr. Patrick Henry is responsible for this resolution concerning the militia," said the tall young St. George Tucker, answering a question. There was quiet in the room as he spoke. "Indeed, it was Mr. Henry and Mr. Henry alone who swayed the convention, persuading them that arms were the only way to make England listen to reason."

"But how did he manage to win Mr. Nicholas and Colonel Bland, and, most of all, Mr. Nelson, the chairman of the council, to his way of thinking?"

"He's a great speaker, Mr. Henry. We all know how he fought the Stamp Act right here in Williamsburg in our own House of Burgesses, and all he used was his own speech-making. But I've never seen him more brilliant than he was in Richmond."

"You were there?" Dr. Galt said eagerly.

"Indeed," Mr. Tucker answered. "I was seated in the gallery of the church and could see the entire proceedings quite clearly."

"Then tell us what he said," came a chorus of voices.

"Well, he began by asking them why they thought Great Britain had a fleet off Boston Harbor. He asked them why they thought Great Britain had troops stationed in Boston. He asked them if our mother country had any other enemy in this part of the world. And of course, the answer is no. This fleet and these soldiers must then be there for use against us alone. Well, then he went on to review our petitions to the king and the Parliament, including those we sent last fall from the convention at Philadelphia.

"Then he just said what he believes: 'The time has come that we must fight!' It was a shock. To many in that church, it was an awful shock to hear that man stand up there and tell them that we must fight against our own brethren, Englishmen against Englishmen. But somehow, it was the way he said it, the great strength of his voice. And his eyes! By heaven, I have never seen eyes like Mr. Henry's when he was making that speech. He laughed at the idea that we were weak and not strong enough to fight Great Britain, and asked:

"'When shall we be stronger? Will it be next week or next year? Will it be when we are totally disarmed and when a British guard shall be stationed in every house? Shall we gather strength by irresolution and inaction?'

"He pointed out that we are not weak if we make proper use of those means which we have at hand. After all, three millions of people armed in the holy cause of liberty and in such a country as ours are invincible, no matter what kind of force our enemy sends against us. How truly he spoke when he said, 'There is no retreat but in submission and slavery.'"

Mr. Tucker stopped speaking a moment. There was silence in the shop. Tom scarcely dared to touch the type for fear he might make a noise in the stillness.

"Gentlemen," Mr. Tucker continued, "you should have heard Mr. Henry as he finished his speech. The very walls of the church seemed to shake and rock. I was sitting where I could see Mr. Henry well; I swear the tendons on his neck stood out white and rigid like whipcord as he said:

"'Our chains are forged, their clanking may be heard on the plains of Boston. The war is inevitable and let it come. Our brethren are already in the field. Why stand we idle? Is life so dear or peace so sweet as to be purchased at the price of chains and slavery?' Then he cried out:

"'Forbid it, Almighty God! I know not what course others may take but for me, give me liberty or give me death!'"

Tom, holding a handful of letters, felt his fingers shake. There was a splatter of type on the floor. Mr. Purdie stood rigid, holding an empty composing stick in his hand. Not a man stirred.

"There was no question when Mr. Henry had finished," Mr. Tucker went on in a quiet voice. "There was no doubt but that the resolution to arm our colony would pass. Mr. Thomas Jefferson had nodded several times to show his sentiments. Colonel Washington sat silent, but it was not hard to tell from his face that he was in complete agreement with the speaker. But the surprise came when it was all over and Mr. Henry had slumped back in his chair. Who do you suppose rose up to speak in his favor? Mr. Nelson, gentlemen, Mr. Nelson, the president of His Majesty's Council, here in Williamsburg, and one of the richest men of the colony, spoke up and declared that, by gad, if British troops were to land about here as they had in Boston, he'd not wait for orders from any man, nor would he obey any order that might attempt to forbid him from summoning up his militia and repelling the invaders at the very water's edge. Well, you can imagine that Mr. Lee did not hesitate to second the resolution as it was passed without a single dissenting vote.

"And that," said Mr. Tucker, smiling, "is how Mr. Henry got his way."

CHAPTER 13

Little more than two weeks had passed since Mr. Patrick Henry made his already famous "liberty or death" speech up in Richmond. Mr. Purdie and Tom had worked night and day to get the report of the convention printed and the Gazette out on time. There was scarcely a day when the office was not the scene of a heated argument or angry words. Tom did his best to try and recall all that was said and which men of the town were most outstanding in these important discussions. All this news he kept stored in his head, trying not to forget a word of it until he had an opportunity, perhaps only late at night when the work of the office was finished, to write Mr. Thruston. Mr. Thruston's letters in reply were full of questions that Tom was hard put to answer, and Mr. Purdie was often called upon to help out when Tom was at a loss for a reply.

It was after writing one of these long letters to his old

friend and teacher that Tom, feeling almost too weary to sleep, took Milly for her usual walk. It was a warm April night and, crossing the Duke of Gloucester Street, they wandered down a side street and turned up the small lane at the back of the Governor's Palace.

Tom, not caring too much which way he went, followed the little white form scampering and sniffing along in front of him. He was deep in the letter he had just written and paid little attention to which way Milly led him, until suddenly he looked up. For some reason the rear gate at the end of the palace garden had been left unlocked. Before Tom realized what had happened, the little dog squeezed herself against the gate just enough that it opened a small crack, and Milly scampered through.

"Milly"—Tom raised his voice slightly—"Milly, you must not go there. Come back. If they catch you, there's no telling what may happen. Who knows what they might do to you? Oh why, oh why did I ever take you for a walk tonight anyway?" Tom whistled eagerly, but the little dog, trotting happily down the wide path between the trim box hedges, did not even look back. She headed straight for the supper room of the palace.

Tom stood hesitating. Should he go after her? The governor was angry and hostile now. Ever since it had been voted to arm and train the militia, he had been suspicious of everyone. There were rumors that he had ordered the marines aboard the armed schooner Magdalen to be on the alert for any trouble in the town. Even a harmless little dog sniffing about in the moonlight in his garden might arouse his anger. Perhaps they would even shoot at her.

"Yet," Tom thought, "there would be even more chance of their catching me if I went in after her. Perhaps it is best to just start home and hope she will follow me."

He turned away from the half-open gate. But, having walked a few steps, he stopped. No, he could not leave Milly in the garden alone. Why, oh why hadn't the gate been securely locked that night as it should have been? Then Milly could never have run into the garden in the first place.

Tom put his hand on the gate and pushed gently. Starting hesitantly up the path, he kept to the shadows of the tall box trees as best he could. Close by the palace he could see a little white form sniffing about the steps that led up to the supper room. The door, being half ajar, revealed the great chandelier with its many candles casting a gentle light in the room and out over the moonlit steps. Coming closer, Tom could see figures moving about inside, and for an instant, he thought he even caught sight of the governor himself, but Tom was too anxious to keep himself in the shadows to try to see more.

Milly, hearing him coming, continued down the path and into the kitchen courtyard. There was a scurrying of feet, and

Tom, pressed close to the wall, watched servants, dressed in fine uniforms, carrying covered platters from the kitchen to the palace. There was the rich smell of good food in the air. No wonder Milly had found her way here.

"Milly!" Tom gasped as the little dog bounced through the half-open door of the kitchen. Tom waited, holding his breath. There was a howl, and angry curse, and Milly came hurtling out, landing with a heavy thud on the brick of the courtyard.

"You ole dog, git outa here. What you all doin' round here anyway?"

A huge cook stood silhouetted in the doorway, threatening Milly with a great wooden ladle. "Try and steal my ducks right off'n the spits, will ya? I'll git the dogs afta you. Git now, befo' I call the dogs."

Tom watched, terrified, as poor Milly picked herself up and, turning, ran past him too fast for him to reach out and catch her. Darting down the path, she headed straight for the dark tunnel of beech trees that led to the end of the garden. Tom sprang forward, whistling softly. He was almost up to the dog when suddenly a black figure appeared at the end of the tunnel. Milly sensed danger before Tom and, turning, raced wildly back down the path. Holding the squirming dog tightly to his side, Tom turned and fled. There were heavy footsteps behind him. Could he get to the back gate of the palace before they caught up with him? Tom realized that the distance was too far. He must hide. He must find some dark thicket or bushes.

Racing through the small box garden, he headed for the fruit garden below. He had only been here once before, when Mr. Purdie sent him with a message to Lord Dunmore. Tom had found the governor walking in the garden showing his little daughter the spring flowers, but he had seen enough so that he recognized where he was, and flinging open the wooden gate at the bottom of the fruit garden, he dove into the maze. Turning to the right instead of the left, as one was supposed to do, he doubled back and forth several times, then slumped to the ground. A sharp thorn from the holly leaves dug into him. They caught Milly's long hair and pulled it. Tom held his hand over her mouth to keep her from whimpering. He lay still in the deep shadows of the high holly hedges. There was the scratching of feet on the gravel path, not running now, but walking fast. Tom heard them circle the maze.

"He will go to the mound behind the maze and try to look down and find me," Tom thought. But he knew he must not move now. Pushing even farther into the hedge, he lay, hardly daring to breathe, while the thorns dug into him and Milly wiggled frantically, trying to escape.

Suddenly there came a short, sharp call.

"I say, are you there?"

A voice from the top of the mound answered.

"Eh, Captain, up here, sir."

"What in heaven's name has got into you?"

"There's somebody in the garden, sir," the voice from the mound answered sullenly.

"Pshaw! Come, come, it's only the governor's good wine that makes you imagine such things. I've been searching the garden for you. The governor has asked for you several times. I've seen nobody. Come down, man. This is no night to be dashing about the garden after imaginary prowlers."

Tom smiled to himself at the reprimand his pursuer was getting. There was the sound of heavy boots on the path. The captain spoke almost angrily as the man came down.

"But I swear," he defended himself, "I swear, Captain, that I saw a small white dog and a figure chasing him. I followed, and now they have disappeared. I felt sure they must have ducked into the maze and be hiding there. After all, we wouldn't want to take any chance tonight of all nights, sir."

The man addressed as captain apparently was too irritated to be influenced by this argument. "Look here," he said with authority, "we've got important work to do tonight for the governor, and I don't want the whole thing thrown off by any talk of mysterious figures and white dogs in the palace garden. Now suppose you hold your addled imagination in check. You're not to mention this to His Lordship, either. Come along."

There was a meek "Yes, sir," then the voices and the footsteps died away.

Tom still hardly dared to move. He ached from lying in a cramped position for so long. But what if they had changed their minds, and the captain was persuaded to return and search the maze after all?

"No," Tom thought wearily, "I'll not be caught after such a narrow escape. I'll just wait a while."

But he did allow himself the luxury of stretching out at full length on the ground for a moment. Then he sat up, drawing his knees tight and squeezing Milly to him; he patted her gently, trying to soothe her injured feelings.

How long he sat there, Tom did not know, but as the chances of his being discovered grew less, he could feel his body relax, his muscles become loose once more. He sat still listening to the night sounds around him: the crackling of the stiff holly leaves, the quacking of the ducks on the canal below the maze, and far away a dog howling sadly at the great full moon.

Then suddenly Tom sat up, stiff and taut. What had happened? Had he been asleep? No, he felt sure he had not, but he felt cold. A wild, sighing wind shook the high hedges, and the dry leaves rattled along the narrow paths of the dark maze. Tom shivered and looked up. A great, billowing mass of black cloud swirled up from nowhere and enveloped the moon. The darkness in the maze was deep and thick and suddenly very lonely.

"Quick, Milly," Tom said, starting up. Milly shook herself. Surely she had been sleeping. "Quick, Milly, now is our chance to escape." Taking her firmly by the neck, Tom opened his shirt and shoved the little dog safely inside, with only her small head showing.

Remembering how he used to run, stealthily, almost Indian-fashion through the woods at home, Tom stooped low and hurried out of the maze. He made his way back through the fruit garden, ducked into the long dark tunnel, and with one dash was at the iron gate at the bottom of the garden.

"What if they have it locked now?" he thought wildly as he approached. But it was easy to see that no watchman had as yet noticed the half-open door, and like a small black shadow in the night, Tom slipped through and pulled the heavy iron gate closed behind him. From there on it was easy. The shadow of the high brick wall made a perfect protection until he should get past the stables and onto the open road and the palace green.

Just as he was beginning to breathe easily again, knowing he had only a short distance more to go, Tom stopped short. There came a strangely familiar sound, but he could not identify it. He stood silent, alert, breathing hard. Could it be, could it possibly be the sound of horses' hoofs on the cobblestones of the palace stable yard? Tom listened again. Then, sliding forward, he came to where he could see the gate in the high brick wall that was used only by the horses and carriages to enter and leave the stable yard.

Tom drew back into the shadow of the wall, for at that moment, the gate opened and two of the governor's black horses appeared pulling a large wagon behind them. Tom could just make out the dark forms of several men crouching low on the seat. The horses' hoofs must have been padded, for they scarcely made a sound even on the cobblestones of the courtyard. When they got to the sandy road that led away from the palace, only the occasional squeak of the wagon wheels could be heard. The gate closed as mysteriously as it had opened, and the dark wagon with its load of silent figures disappeared into the blackness of the night.

CHAPTER 14

Tom heard a dull thudding, not clearly at first, only far away as if in a dream. Stirring uneasily, he tried to escape the noise by putting his head under the pillow. The sound grew louder. Tom knew now that this was no dream. It was a drum being beaten in the street below. Leaping out of bed, he hurried to the window. It was early gray dawn outside, for the sun had not yet risen, but in this half light, Tom could make out a cluster of men gathered by the steps of the Raleigh Tavern. A militiaman patrolled back and forth in the street, beating monotonously on a huge drum hanging from his shoulder.

Then Tom saw. Tom saw that the men were armed. Nearly

every man carried a musket. What was the matter? Had something terrible happened in the town during the night? In the night? Tom remembered! He remembered what he had seen at the palace gates the night before—perhaps it was only a few hours before, he was not sure—but he felt that there must be some connection between this gathering of armed men, this beating of the ominous drum, and the wagon he had seen drive mysteriously away from the palace.

Hurrying into his clothes, he was soon on the Duke of Gloucester Street. The sun was beginning to cast a pink light on the houses and reflect on the faces of the crowd, giving the men a strange, flushed look of anger.

The street was becoming more crowded all the time. Men were arriving on horseback, on foot, and some even in their chariots. House doors were being thrown open, and the faces of women looked anxiously from the windows. At first, Tom could not find anyone he knew, but, pushing his way into the center of the group, he saw a tall figure and recognized Dr. Galt almost immediately in front of him.

"Dr. Galt," Tom said, tugging at his sleeve, "what is it, sir?"

The doctor turned, his face grave and taut. "Ah, Tom, you've not heard? It's the magazine."

"The magazine?" Tom questioned.

"The powder was removed from the magazine in the night. It's Lord Dunmore who ordered it."

So that was what the wagon was for—the explanation flashed through Tom's mind.

"Eh, the arrogant old fool thinks he can rob us of our gunpowder and firearms, and in this way control us." Looking back, Tom saw that it was the burly blacksmith's journeyman who had spoken.

"But why?" Tom turned once more to the doctor. Before he could get an answer, the journeyman bellowed over the heads of the crowd:

"We should march on the palace. March on His Lordship. Let's show him he can't rob us."

There was an angry growl from the gathering in reply. Before he knew what was happening, Tom was being shoved forward with the ever-growing crowd. He was pushed from behind. Dr. Galt reached out, trying to hold him by the arm, but the press of the crowd was too strong for him, and the two were jostled, shoved, and hurried along as if caught in a fast-running stream.

It was not until they were opposite the magazine that the crowd slowed a little. Many broke away, and for a moment, forgetting the errand they were on, collected in small knots about the high wall that guarded the little peaked-roof building that had always been used for the storing of guns and powder. Then, once more, there was a surge forward, but this time toward the courthouse. Tom, looking eagerly to see what had drawn the crowd together again, saw two figures standing on the top step of the square brick courthouse. He pressed forward with the others.

The taller of the two men raised his arm in the air. Recognizing Mr. Peyton Randolph, Tom wondered how the man could possibly hope to control such angry people. But no sooner had he begun to speak than there was quiet, and everywhere the little thud, thud of muskets being rested on the ground. The people pushed forward, shoving one against another, shushing those who still grumbled too loudly.

"People of Williamsburg," Mr. Randolph began, and from

the very first words, it was easy to understand why he had been chosen president of the Continental Congress at Philadelphia. The man spoke quietly, and yet with such force and command that even the restless sound of many feet shuffling on the hard ground stopped. In the clear early morning light, with the new sun sharp in his face, Mr. Randolph pleaded, "People of Williamsburg, it is true what you have discovered. All the powder has been removed from the magazine. And you are quite right in supposing that it is our governor, Lord Dunmore, who has ordered this to be carried out. Nevertheless, although you have every right to be angry, I beg of you, do not let us lose sight of reason. We are common God-fearing men, not hoodlums and hotheads."

"So we are to sit idly by and let him trick and rob us?" the burly blacksmith's journeyman roared from the crowd. Many heads turned in the man's direction. Several tried to take him by the arm and remove him from the group, but moving that great giant was like trying to move a small mountain. Seeing that he had so easily gained himself an audience, he would not give up too quickly. He was obviously a man whose talk was as big as his frame.

"I say we are chicken-livered," he bawled again at the top of his rough voice. "Weaklings, muling, puking babies if we let him do this to us and without protest. Let us find out where the powder lies, and we'll bring it back ourselves."

"Eh, he's right. Where is the powder? Let us fetch it," cried several in the crowd. Some lifted their muskets once more, but Mr. Randolph stood firm and took no notice of the interruption.

"There is no need for action now," he continued. "Already a protest and inquiry have been sent to His Lordship. He has already admitted that he requested Lieutenant Collins, whom you all have seen on these very streets and know is the commander of the armed schooner Magdalen, which now lies in the James, to convey the powder aboard the Fowey, anchored in the York River. So you see, it would be impossible for us to retrieve it now. Lieutenant Collins and his men only did as they were ordered, carrying away the powder in the governor's wagon."

"Down with Lord Dunmore! Down with Collins!" Several in the crowd took up the ominous chant. The blacksmith had by this time managed to make himself the leader of a small group of rough-looking men who pushed forward toward the steps where Mr. Randolph stood alone and unprotected. Tom could barely make out the huge frame of the journeyman about to shove his way up the steps, when suddenly a lithe, strong figure stepped in front of him.

"It's Mr. Lee," Tom gasped. "It's Mr. Richard Henry Lee. I can tell by the black handkerchief he wears on that injured hand of his. He's stopping the blacksmith." Tom was relaying the events to a knot of men who had been pushed behind a huge tree and were unable to see what was happening on the steps of the courthouse. "Mr. Lee is protesting that the men should not come any closer. Mr. Lee is protecting Mr. Randolph from that brute of a blacksmith."

"That man has less brains than the horses he shoes," a man close to Tom said in disgust.

Just then a short, handsome figure sprang up the steps and stood, arms outstretched, pleading once more for silence.

"Mr. Robert Carter Nicholas," Tom whispered as he recognized the elegant gentleman who came often to the shop to inquire for the latest news brought by the post rider.

"The great gentleman speaks," bellowed the sneering voice of the blacksmith.

"Friends." Mr. Nicholas spoke smoothly, and Tom felt the crowd ease back for Mr. Nicholas, for although he had at times been called a too-hardy patriot, he was beloved by the people and trusted by them. He had the charm of the Carters and the Nicholases combined in great measure.

"Friends," he began again, "don't think we have not already been to the governor for an explanation. Indeed, we have sent a message asking by what right and for what reason he has emptied the magazine as if it were his property and not ours? Now his answer has just arrived. A verbal answer it is, and Mr. Lee has just brought it from the palace himself."

The long, lean figure of Mr. Lee stood erect and calm as he looked over the crowd. They knew Mr. Richard Henry Lee well as being one of their supporters at all times. He spoke with enthusiasm.

"Yes, 'tis right," he began. "I have been to the palace already this morning and held conference with His Lordship concerning what happened in the night. I have talked long and earnestly with him, and he assured me that he meant no harm to our town by the taking of the powder. He explained to me that he feared an insurrection of the slaves in Surry County. He wished to have the powder out of harm's way, and ordered it removed in the night so as not to alarm us."

Voices growled. Fists clenched and waved in the air. Men were shaking their heads. This was not enough. This was mere talk.

"And when, pray, may we expect the return of our powder?" a voice roared angrily from the opposite side of the street.

Ignoring the tone of the question, Mr. Lee responded. "He has promised, upon his word of honor, that it shall be returned within half an hour whenever any danger threatens us."

Tom looked anxiously about him. He had never forgotten the arrogant face of Lord Dunmore as he had driven too swiftly through the streets, and the heartless disregard for what he had done to Milly and almost to Tom himself. It was not hard to guess that these words from a man of such character as Lord Dunmore meant little.

"I beg of you, good people of Williamsburg," Mr. Randolph pleaded once more, "I implore you, do not let this matter cause us to indulge in any hurried action which we would all soon regret."

Tom, standing once more on tip-toe, looked over the crowd. There was a nodding of heads for the most part. Only the small knot about the blacksmith seemed unconvinced, and as Tom was wondering how Mr. Randolph would handle them, he felt a tug at his sleeve.

"Tom, Tom."

Turning, Tom saw the anxious face of Mr. Purdie, who was standing beside him. "Come, Tom, the Gazette. There must be a supplement as quickly as possible with these events. Quick, Tom, I need you."

Reluctantly, Tom turned and, elbowing his way through the close-packed men, followed his master back to the office. As he hurried up the steps to the door, he looked back down the street and could see that the crowd was already beginning to break up. Some were searching out their horses in the market square, while others passed the shop windows, walking slowly, thoughtfully home again.

CHAPTER 15

On the nineteenth of April, 1775, there was fighting at Concord and Lexington in the faraway colony of Massachusetts. There was fighting and bloodshed when the British regulars tried to go off with the colonists' powder and the stout farmers of Concord and Lexington decided to stop them.

"That's terrible news, Tom." Mr. Purdie stood in the flickering candlelight reading the letters that had just arrived from the Committee of Safety in Philadelphia.

Tom was bewildered. "What does this mean? When did it happen?"

"Just nine days ago, Tom. It happened on almost the same night as our gunpowder was taken. Thank heaven for Mr. Randolph, Mr. Nicholas, and Mr. Lee. If they hadn't done what they did in putting sense into some of those hotheads who were all for marching direct to the palace, we might easily have had bloodshed in Williamsburg, too."

Tom worked all night printing the broadside with the news from Concord and Lexington. It had arrived too late for the regular edition of the Gazette which had just been delivered, so Mr. Purdie decided on a special sheet to carry the news. All night they worked, and by morning the great pile, with the ink still wet on the sheets, was ready for Tom to deliver.

His heavy bundle slung over his shoulder, he hurried out of the shop. He was tired. His arms and back ached, and his eyes were red from the long hours of work by candlelight. Starting toward the Capitol, where he was in the habit of delivering the first copy of the Gazette each Friday morning, Tom passed the apothecary shop just as Dr. Galt was unlocking the door for the morning.

"Why, Tom," the older man said looking up in surprise. "Why are you delivering papers on Saturday? Didn't I receive mine only yesterday?" He hesitated, and Tom could feel that he was being examined in a most professional manner. "Tom, Tom, what is the matter?" the doctor said anxiously. "You look sick, boy, as if you'd not slept all night. What is it? Is anything wrong?"

Tom felt embarrassed and hardly knew how to answer. His voice sounded hoarse and deep when he spoke. "Well, yes, sir, there is trouble," he managed to stammer at last. "We've been working all night at the shop. There's bad news, Dr. Galt, bad news from the colony of Massachusetts. There's been fighting."

"Fighting? You mean, boy—" the doctor began, then stopped as Tom slipped a copy of the special sheet from his bundle and pointed to the letters from Philadelphia.

Dr. Galt read hastily, and Tom, somehow fascinated to hear the words he had worked so long and hard to put into print, could not seem to move on. He stood listening.

"TO ALL FRIENDS OF AMERICAN LIBERTY: BE IT KNOWN THAT THIS MORNING BEFORE BREAK OF DAY, A BRIGADE, CONSISTING OF ABOUT 1,000 OR 1,200 MEN LANDED AT PHIPPS FARM AT CAMBRIDGE AND MARCHED TO LEXINGTON, WHERE THEY FOUND A COMPANY OF OUR COLONY MILITIA IN ARMS, UPON WHOM THEY FIRED WITHOUT ANY PROVOCATION AND KILLED SIX MEN AND WOUNDED FOUR OTHERS. BY EXPRESS MESSENGER FROM BOSTON WE FIND

ANOTHER BRIGADE IS NOW ON ITS MARCH FROM
BOSTON SUPPOSED TO CONSIST OF 1,000 MEN."

When he had ended the letter, the doctor stood silent a
moment, then read what Mr. Purdie himself had seen fit to add:

"IS IT NOT FULL TIME FOR US ALL TO BE ON OUR
GUARD AND TO PREPARE OURSELVES AGAINST EVERY
CONTINGENCY? THE SWORD IS NOW DRAWN AND
GOD KNOWS WHEN IT WILL BE SHEATHED."

The tall, slim figure stood without moving as he finished his
reading. He repeated Mr. Purdie's words over and over, half to
himself, half aloud. "'The sword is now drawn and God knows
when it will be sheathed.'"

"Dr. Galt." Tom hardly dared interrupt the other man's
thoughts. "Sir, do you think we're really going to have war, sir?"

The doctor looked down and smiled. "I don't know, Tom. I
honestly don't know. We might have had bloodshed right here
in Williamsburg barely ten days ago, when the crowd gathered
by the courthouse and wanted to march on the governor. They
say the militias of Spotsylvania and Caroline are still anxious to
come into Williamsburg and force the return of the powder. I
understand that Colonel Washington himself has been asked to
lead the group. But still I don't think that will come to anything.
Mr. Randolph has just dispatched a letter to the leaders
explaining the whole matter more clearly. Still"—the tall, grave
doctor hesitated—"I suppose the militias of Spotsylvania and
Caroline are not too different from those of Concord and
Lexington when they are roused."

"But—but you really don't think they would fight here?" Tom
stopped, looked about him, and finished. "I mean right here, sir,
right on the Duke of Gloucester Street or on the palace green?"

"No, Tom, I don't think so now, but"—the doctor

hesitated—"but if any other hothead takes it upon himself to protest the actions of the governor, well, who knows, we could have some blows. Lord Dunmore is in no mood for trifling. These are troubled times, Tom."

The man turned and put his key back into the lock. Tom started on. "Wait," the good doctor called after him. "Here, boy, eat these while you walk. They'll taste good and give you a bit of strength, too."

Tom was delighted as he held out his hand for the almond comfits and barley sugar that Dr. Galt poured into it. They were Tom's favorite sweets.

Three days passed. The excitement of the news from Massachusetts had subsided, and a feeling of thankful security returned to the town. The weather was warm now, with the soft winds and the hot sun of early May. Perhaps it was this that helped in part to lull the town back into peace so quickly. Even at the printing office Mr. Purdie himself seemed less worried than he had been for some time. At the beginning of the week, he had told Tom that he did not consider it safe for him to ride out to the nearby plantations on Friday to deliver the Gazette. This expedition had become, by a sort of unwritten agreement between Tom and his master, a form of day off for Tom, and he looked forward to the leisurely ride through the countryside on the big chestnut mare. But now after three days of calm and peace, Mr. Purdie relented, and Tom started off as usual with a bundle of papers tied securely in a large leather pouch slung across the saddle.

At each stopping place he was questioned eagerly as to what new development there was in Williamsburg, but aside from this unusual cross-questioning, Tom saw and heard little that could be considered alarming. He returned at his own pace thinking mostly of the chicken corn pie and sweet potato buns old Betty had promised to make for him. It was not until he was almost at the Purdie's house that he noticed anything wrong with the town. What was that large gathering of men outside the Raleigh Tavern? Was Tom mistaken, or were there an unusual number of carriages and chariots in the streets?

Quickly tying his horse to the Purdie's hitching post, he leapt up the steps to the porch, hesitating only a moment to look at the men hurriedly coming and going from the King's Arms next door. As he stepped into the house, he was stopped abruptly by a great barricade of bags, trunks, and packages all piled in confusion about the hall.

At the sound of the door opening, Miss Peachy called from upstairs, "Tom, Tom, is that you?"

"Yes," Tom answered, bewildered.

"Come up this minute. I have something to tell you." Miss Peachy's voice was impatient and anxious.

As Tom hurried up the stairs, he was almost knocked over by Alice scuttling by him laden down with the boys' clothes. As she passed him, she gave Tom a look of important mystery. Close behind her trailed little Billy, her five-year-old son.

"Is they comin', is they comin' to shoot us, Ma?" he wailed.

"Stop that ridiculous sniffling, Billy," Miss Peachy ordered sharply from her room.

Tom entered hesitantly. There were more boxes and packages everywhere. Drawers were half open, and the closet stood empty. Alex and William slouched on a small sofa in one corner. Miss Peachy turned quickly, and Tom thought he had never seen her look so worried and tired.

"Come in, Tom." There was a tone of command in her voice that Tom had never heard before. "We have been waiting anxiously for you. There is not time to mince words. Mr. Purdie has received word that Mr. Henry is marching on Williamsburg."

"Marching, marching on Williamsburg!" Tom gasped.

"It's all to do with the taking of the gunpowder, Tom. You know as much about all this dreadful business as I do. Mr. Henry believes it should be returned right away and has decided he'll come himself with a large band of men and see to it. Oh, the fool, the—the—" Miss Peachy started walking hurriedly up and down, twisting her linen handkerchief nervously in her hands. "There's no telling what may happen now. Alexander is wild. He's decided it's not safe for us here. We must go. The two boys and I are to go to my cousin's plantation up the river. Oh, the fool! The fool! After what happened at Concord and Lexington, I should think Mr. Henry would move more slowly. They say His Lordship is frightfully angry and will do anything, anything to stop him."

"I won't go." William jumped up and faced his mother defiantly. "If there's going to be fighting, I want to see it."

"Indeed, you will go, young man," Miss Peachy said, wheeling on her son, her eyes blazing.

"Is Tom going, too?" William challenged again.

"No, your father needs him at the shop. Besides, don't forget that Tom is older and quite used to taking care of himself. In fact, I've no doubt he could handle a gun far better than most men in town."

Tom flushed at this unexpected compliment, but nevertheless was relieved that he was not going to be forced to leave with the others.

"Ooo, thar's goin' to be shootin'," a small voice wailed from the doorway, and despite her worry and haste, Miss Peachy couldn't hold back a smile at the woebegone face of little Billy, who sat hugging himself while tears of fright streamed down his shiny brown face. Alex said nothing, but, sliding quietly from his chair, he sidled up to Miss Peachy and, taking her hand, he held it shyly behind him. He was not the adventurer that his brother was, or young enough to show his fear openly, like little Billy.

The bustle in the house seemed to increase by the minute. The boys were allowed to gather up their most beloved possessions. Miss Peachy gave orders to old Betty, who had come in from the kitchen.

"You are to feed Mr. Purdie, Tom, and young James well, Betty. None of your laziness now, just because I am not here to fret." Miss Peachy smiled, and old Betty's grin was all the assurance anyone needed that she would do all in her power to keep the "menfolk" quite happy.

Tom listened eagerly. So James was not to go with his mother. Tom had wondered about that. No doubt he had refused to be carted away with the women and children.

At last the time came. John had the carriage at the door, the trunks and bags were stored carefully inside and on the top. Miss Peachy, Alex, William, Alice, and little Billy, bawling now like a stuck pig, climbed in and made themselves as comfortable as they could with so many bags to share the small space with them. John cracked his whip and shouted, "Geddap, hola!" importantly. The carriage shook and moved. Miss Peachy leaned out of the window and waved an already damp handkerchief until they had made the turn by the Capitol. Now only the slowly settling dust was left to the little group gathered on the Purdie house steps.

CHAPTER 16

There was an unrest, suspicion, and fear in the town now. Each person questioned what position his neighbor would take. Would he side with the governor or would he join the rebels and fight with Mr. Patrick Henry? Windows were barricaded. Families drove off in well-curtained carriages, and it was common knowledge that Lady Dunmore and her three children had fled in the night to the safety of the man-of-war, Fowey, to remain under the protection of Captain Montague and his "boiled crabs," as the red-coated marines were now called.

Tom saw with his own eyes the cannons His Lordship had ordered to be placed about the palace and inside the gates. There was a rumor that every servant went armed night and day, and that His Lordship was so angry that he had even threatened to burn the whole town to the ground, if need be, to bring the townspeople to what he termed "their senses."

Mr. Purdie had the shutters of his house closed and locked securely, and Tom spent most of his time, when not in the office, out in the kitchen with old Betty, watching her stoop into the great fireplace, bending over her big iron kettles and turning the spits with the chickens and meats she roasted each day for the three men of the house.

At the shop it was almost impossible for any work to be done, for the place was filled all day and often well into the night with people waiting for news. But only rumor continued to flow into town: Mr. Henry had near a thousand men; Mr. Henry threatened to shoot His Lordship on sight; Mr. Henry was so enraged at the actions of the governor that he would no doubt burn the palace the very moment he arrived in town. Muskets that had grown rusty by too long a sojourn in town were brought out and cleaned. Men who had shot nothing but an occasional partridge for many years were heard practicing at sunset in the woods outside the town.

Mr. Purdie loaned Tom a musket and told him to sleep with it close to his bed. "Just in case, Tom. His Lordship bears me no good will. I've published letters of his that he would just as soon nobody saw on this side of the ocean. He might get the idea that Mr. Purdie's Gazette could be dispensed with, and now would be as good a time as any to do it. He did not care for my remark after the news of Concord and Lexington that 'The sword is now drawn and God knows when it will be sheathed.' They say he's planning to arrest Mr. Henry as a rebel as soon as he can lay hands on him."

The night after Mrs. Purdie and the boys left the house, there was the tramp of heavy feet up the Duke of Gloucester Street, and a group of marines, ordered from the river by the governor, were openly paraded to the palace. Surly, angry faces watched from behind half-closed shutters, and small boys dared to throw a few rocks at the stiff, marching figures.

Tom hated the sullen silence that prevailed throughout the

town. He watched anxiously as messenger after messenger was dispatched to Mr. Henry, who, it was learned, had by this time been made Captain Henry by his followers. But to no avail; Captain Henry merely detained the messengers and continued his march.

"They say he's scarce sixteen miles from town now. I know 'tis true, for my son has just ridden there and back again." Old Mr. Jones, being one of the few still loyal to the governor, spoke angrily to those gathered in the shop. "By gad, they should send out and hang the man. They say he's set himself up at Doncastle's Ordinary and dispatched a young man, Ensign Parke Goodall, with sixteen men to Laneville to force three hundred and thirty pounds, in payment for the powder, out of our Receiver General, Mr. Corbin."

"Eh, Mr. Jones." Mr. Purdie stopped work at the type case and came around to face the old man. "Eh, they say if Mr. Corbin does not get orders from the governor to pay this sum, he'll be taken prisoner, and Captain Henry will march straight into Williamsburg and demand the powder, or payment, back from the governor in person."

"Rebels, rebels, I say, and, by gad, it would give me pleasure to shoot him on sight."

Tom watched anxiously. Mr. Purdie, looking pale and tired from two days of anxious waiting, flushed suddenly with anger.

"Mr. Jones," he answered calmly enough, "I have a high respect for Captain"—he put careful emphasis on the new title—"Henry, and I do not care to have such talk against him in my shop. If, sir, it is necessary for you to express your contrary feelings in such a manner, then I must ask you to express them in some other place than my office."

Tom was amazed. Mr. Purdie asking Mr. Jones to leave! The
door slammed with such force that Tom dropped the type he
was distributing and spent the next hour on his hands and
knees collecting it.

On the third morning, there seemed to be a new excitement
in the air. Lights had burned late in the palace. Messengers
had pounded up and down the Duke of Gloucester Street
several times in the night. All during the day men came and
went in the shop, talking in hushed voices, discussing rumors
and attempting to bolster one another's spirits. Tom thought
he could not stand the suspense any longer. He almost wished
Captain Henry would come. Anything would be better than this
endless watching and waiting.

Toward evening the tension was at its height, and there was a
mounting feeling that something must happen before morning.
Would it be the sound of marching feet coming around the turn

by the Capitol? Would it be the news that His Lordship had swallowed his pride and agreed to pay Captain Henry?

The answer came at last. It came with the sound of a great black horse galloping up the Duke of Gloucester Street toward the palace.

"Quick, Tom," Mr. Purdie cried, hurrying to the half-open door of the shop. "There he goes! There he goes, young Carter Braxton returning from Captain Henry at Doncastle's Ordinary. He carried the governor's offer of payment to Captain Henry, and now he is returning."

Tom and Mr. Purdie stood on the steps watching. "See, he's turning down the palace green now. In a moment, he'll be giving the news to His Lordship." Mr. Purdie chuckled to himself. "He'll be giving the news that Captain Henry has been paid three hundred and thirty pounds by the Receiver General and is now marching peacefully home."

How the news spread so fast nobody knew, but with the passing of the anxious young rider on his fast galloping horse, the whole town knew there would be no fighting in Williamsburg. Men flooded out into the streets. Windows that had been barred and shutters that had been locked were again opened. Well-oiled muskets and pistols were returned to their cases once more.

CHAPTER 17

On the eighth day of June, 1775, the people of Williamsburg woke to find themselves in possession of a well-fortified but quite empty palace. His Lordship had departed in the dark hours before dawn, seeking refuge on the man-of-war Fowey.

This was startling news. Captain Henry had made his bold stand on the matter of the gunpowder little more than a month before. Had he so frightened His Lordship that he dared try the patience of his colonists no longer? Had Captain Henry so impressed His Majesty's servant that he felt it safer to uphold the king's rule from the protection of a British man-of-war?

The news spread fast through the town, and there were many who could not restrain a sly grin at the bravery of His Lordship. A curious crowd gathered outside the gates of the palace. But there was no disorder, no unseemly behavior, no outward show of hostility. But there was questioning and wondering. Who will be governor now? Will the Crown dare send us another?

But the months that were to follow would answer enough of these questions. His Lordship soon gave up all efforts to rule from his ship and by the end of summer decided to make war on his colonists instead. Even this proved rather unsatisfactory, and at last the unhappy man sailed away home, leaving the government of the colony to the Virginia Convention. This body appointed a Committee of Safety, who in turn promoted Captain Henry to Colonel Henry, and made him Commander-in-Chief of all Virginia forces, with headquarters in Williamsburg.

Up north in Philadelphia, the Second Continental Congress was also making appointments. On the second of July, Colonel George Washington was made a general and chief of all troops "raised for the defense of American liberty." And at the Battle of Bunker Hill, the colonists showed the British and General Howe that the "rebels" were worth taking notice of. A great surge of courage swept through the colonies.

The summer of 1775 passed hot and still in the little capital of Williamsburg. News from up north was waited for eagerly, and Mr. Purdie's Gazette was looked to for the latest information there was to be had. Tom and his master worked through long days and sultry nights, reading the reports, the letters, and any other gazettes they could lay hands on. Tom longed to have more of a chance in the actual printing of these reports, but still Mr. Purdie clung to his rule that he, and he alone, would set the type for all important political material.

"It's in no way a criticism of you, Tom," Mr. Purdie said gently, knowing Tom's ambitions. "It's just that we can't afford to take chances. If there is a mistake, then let it be on my shoulders and not yours."

So Tom had to accept his status of ink mixer, sweeper of floors, clerk for the books and music, and setter of type only for the ads concerning runaway slaves or notices of purses snatched or dropped in some ordinary. Tom chafed under these restrictions. He felt so sure, so confident that he could set type as well and as accurately as any man, even his master, but he knew that there was little he could do, so he tended the business that was given him and tried hard not to complain.

By fall, Henry had his troops quartered outside the town

at Waller's Grove and was able to put on a parade with some
semblance of military order as he rode at the front of Virginia's
force, while his loyal supporters tramped behind with "Liberty
or Death" emblazoned on their shirt fronts.

The winter came and with it a new word for the colonists.
It was a word that had only been muttered before, a word men
had thought about, perhaps, but when Mr. Tom Paine wrote his
new book, Common Sense, the word "Independence" came into
the open.

Mr. Purdie printed large sections of Paine's book in the
Gazette, running it through most of the month of January.
By the time spring came once more to Williamsburg,
"Independence" was the word on every man's lips and the hope
in many men's hearts.

Tom looked forward to his second spring in Williamsburg. It
was hard for him to believe he had been there a full year. It was
hard for him still to believe that he had learned as much as he
had. He was very happy in his work, and he was happy outside
of it in all ways but one, and that one was a worry to him.

Shortly after the winter season had passed and all the
crocuses, anemones, and daffodils had come and gone once
more, a letter arrived from Mr. Thruston, telling Tom of his
mother's sickness.

"Would it be possible, my boy," the letter ended
questioningly, "for you to send a small sum of money to your
mother? Am I mistaken in thinking that she gave you a little
when you left for Williamsburg? Perhaps this is none of my
affair, Tom, but your mother is in dire need of money."

Tom put the letter down slowly. When his mother entrusted
him with the money, there had been little doubt in Tom's mind

that he would be able to return at least part of it to her long
before this. But the robbery had made this impossible, and the
small wages he received from Mr. Purdie he had been forced to
use for the few daily needs of his own life. Tom could think of
nothing but his mother. As he "twisted the devil's tail," pulling
impression after impression of the Gazette from the press, he
was haunted by the vision of her lying sick and unattended
except for Milly, whom Tom knew could be of little help at her
age. Should he give up his apprenticeship and return home?
Should he ask for time off from his work? Tom turned these
possible solutions over and over in his mind as he worked.
He knew he would be of little help in tending a sick woman,
and there was little chance of his being able to earn money in
the back country. No, if he were to make money, he'd best stay
where he was and find jobs at night when his work in the office
was over. Besides, Tom knew all too well now that Mr. Purdie
could never carry on the work in the shop by himself. Although
he never admitted it himself, Miss Peachy had confided to Tom,
her husband was not well. At times it was almost impossible
for him to hold the composing stick in his hand to set type,
and Tom watched in an agony of hope that Mr. Purdie might at
last trust him enough to turn over at least part of the political
reports to him to set. But Mr. Purdie was adamant. More and
more small articles fell to Tom, but any of importance Mr.
Purdie set up and hovered over like an anxious old hen.

March passed and April came with its showers and hot days
that brought the glistening white and pink patches of dogwood
to the gardens and woods. Mr. Purdie worked mercilessly,
and Tom strained to do all he could, but his heart was not in
his work for the first time since he had come to the shop. Mr.
Purdie noticed this at last and questioned him about it.

"You're not sick, Tom?" he asked, watching his apprentice

wearily throw the great bundle of Gazettes over his shoulder in preparation for his usual Friday rounds.

Tom started at this question, for he had no desire to reveal his new problem to his employer. The secret of the stolen purse was one that Tom and Miss Peachy had guarded for a year, and Tom did not want Mr. Purdie to learn of it now. As to his mother's illness, Tom said nothing on that score either, knowing full well Mr. Purdie would offer to furnish any funds that were necessary, and Tom was too proud for that.

"Oh no, sir, I'm in fine health. I'm sorry if I'm not doing well." Tom looked up anxiously. "It's just the sudden heat, maybe." He wiped his forehead jerkily with his sleeve and hurried out of the door.

The papers seemed heavier than ever this morning, and Tom was glad enough to be through with his delivery as he approached the courthouse, where he always left the few Gazettes that remained at the end of his route. Stopping to examine the notices and advertisements posted outside the door and to gossip a moment with the crowd that was always collected there in the sunshine, Tom noticed a group of boys gathered eagerly in front of a large announcement. Pushing forward to join them, he was hailed by several of his friends.

"Now here's Tom," one said. "Will you run in the race, Tom?"

"Are you soft from typesetting?" asked another.

"I'll warrant he could have run faster than any boy in town when he first came. But look at him now, all dressed in fine clothes and fat as a pig," they joked.

Tom only grinned good-naturedly at these friendly jibes, for he'd learned in his year in town to take city jokes, and besides, he saw the smiles and could not but notice the approving looks of several of the speakers as they inspected him slyly.

"A race, eh?" He read half aloud, "There is to be no fair on St. George's Day this year because of the unsettled condition existing in our colony. However, the various contests will be held as usual," Tom read on. "A foot race is to be run from the college to the Capitol, the length of a good mile. The winner to receive a pair of fine silver buckles worth twenty shillings."

"Well, Tom, why not?" Tom turned to see the kindly, smiling face of his friend Dr. Galt looking down at him.

"I've no time, sir," Tom smiled back. "We're too busy at the shop."

"Come, come," the doctor said, chuckling and looking searchingly at Tom. "A little fresh air and exercise would do you good. Besides, think what a dandy you'd be with fine silver buckles to wear on your rounds with the Gazette."

This brought a laugh from the crowd, and Tom felt himself going crimson. With that, Dr. Galt took a pencil from his pocket and added "Tom Cartwright" to the list of names already affixed to the placard.

Tom thought little of the incident as he returned to the shop, and as for the race and his chances of winning a pair of silver buckles, this seemed even more ridiculous. He had too many other problems to worry about a contest in running. No further mention was made of the incident until barely two weeks before the race was to be held. Tom was alone in the shop setting type. Bending over the type cases, he was unaware that anyone had entered the shop, until suddenly, looking up, he saw James Purdie standing in the doorway. Taking it for granted that the boy was looking for his father, Tom informed him that Mr. Purdie was attending a meeting at the Raleigh Tavern and would not return that morning.

"Never mind about my father." James' tone was surly. Tom looked at him in surprise. What possible message could James have for Tom? They never spoke except to exchange the necessary formalities at the Purdie house, and the idea of young James seeking him out to talk to him in the shop seemed strange to Tom.

"I see you fancy yourself as a runner," James said, coming close to the type cases.

Tom gripped his composing stick hard. Now what could this possibly mean? "And why, may I ask, does that worry you?" he snapped. Surely the skinny little dandy had no intention of entering the competition himself.

"It doesn't." James, coming around the type cases, stood close to Tom. He spoke low. His voice sounded tense. "But this is just a warning. I wouldn't run if I were you. It might be bad for your health, you know."

Tom looked up at the squinting little eyes, the surly curled lips drawn tightly together, and he saw the soft white hand nervously twirling an expensive gold watch fob. "What are you talking about?" Tom's scorn for the boy was so great that he found it difficult to speak to him civilly at any time, much less now.

"I'm not talking about anything. I'm just giving you fair warning that I would remove my name from that race as soon as possible if I were you."

"But thank heaven you're not," Tom muttered half out loud, half to himself.

"All right." James sauntered back toward the open door. "Just remember I've warned you that you might be a healthier man if you decided not to race."

Tom laughed quietly to himself as he watched the elegant figure cross the Duke of Gloucester Street and enter the Raleigh Tavern.

"That settles it, my fine friend," he thought. "Of course I had no intention of entering the race, but since it seems to mean so much to you, then race I will. But why in heaven's name does it mean so much to you?"

While he worked, Tom puzzled, and the more he puzzled, the more resolved he became that he would not remove his name from the list of entries at the courthouse. Suddenly Tom laid down his composing stick. The words of the placard came back to him: "The winner to receive a pair of fine silver buckles worth twenty shillings."

"Twenty shillings," thought Tom. "Twenty shillings is worth racing for. My mother could use twenty shillings, I feel sure."

From that moment on, for the next two weeks Tom could think of nothing but the race. Asking to be let off from work early each night, he took to the woods. Poor Milly, trailing along the hot sandy road, was bewildered at this unaccustomed activity on the part of her master, but followed along, happily glad of an opportunity to leave the tiny room where she was forced to spend most of her evenings.

Barely a quarter of a mile from town was a stretch of road seldom traveled, and this was Tom's practice ground. Pulling off his stock and shirt, and stripping to the waist, he ran up and down the road. Going slowly at first, he increased his speed until each evening he felt as if he had made a little progress. His muscles began to feel strong, his breath came more easily, and he was quicker at the start.

Little Milly watched all this peculiar behavior with mixed delight and disgust. She welcomed the opportunity for more walks, but thought that this dashing off up the road and sudden startings and stoppings of their walk quite spoiled the fun. By the end of two weeks, on Tom's last evening of practice, she renounced her master entirely and went off into the deeper woods on her own rabbit expedition.

It was growing dark, and Tom lay stretched on the soft pine needles under the tall pines that lined the road. He knew it was no use, in fact dangerous, to try running in the dark. The road was rough, and he might easily fall, twisting an ankle or otherwise injuring himself, and thus spoiling every chance for the race. He had a sudden confidence in himself now, having gone over the list of the competitors again. The only one he felt uneasy about was Jake, the mountain of a blacksmith.

"The man is heavy," thought Tom, "but I've watched him with the horses, and, by gad, he's as spry as any man half his size. If only he doesn't get in front of me. I'd never get around that great hulk."

Tom sat up suddenly. Surely there was the crackling of a twig in the darkness of the woods across the road. Tom listened. A small bird fluttered from branch to branch overhead.

"Milly, Milly, is that you?" Tom called softly, but there was no sound of the little dog. Then suddenly Tom was on his feet. He retreated a few steps. There was no mistaking it now. Two dark figures were coming quickly toward him through the woods.

CHAPTER 18

"So there you are, my fine friend." The larger of the two figures broke through the underbrush. But it was not until he stood on the opposite side of the narrow dirt road that Tom could make out who it was. Jake, the great, burly blacksmith, stood heaving, puffing, and angry, with none other than James Purdie swaggering safely behind him.

"Well, good evening," Tom said as calmly as the sudden appearance of these two unwelcome visitors would allow. "This is—well, I mean I hadn't expected to see you two around here."

The blacksmith took a step forward. Tom noticed for the first time that he held a long ugly horsewhip partially concealed behind him.

"No doubt it's a bit of a surprise," he said. The hairy chest of the huge man made a great black scar down his half-open white shirt front. "But we've come to give you a warning, Tom Cartwright. James here says he's already given you one before. Forget about that race tomorrow."

"Race!" Tom gasped. Slowly the meaning of this sudden intrusion dawned on him. "You mean running the race tomorrow? You don't want me to run?"

"Now there's a smart lad." The blacksmith stood halfway across the road, his legs wide apart, his huge fist grasping the long whip, and a slight sneer twisting his thick lips.

Tom held his ground on the other side of the road. "And what, may I ask, has all this got to do with the pair of you?"

"Never you mind, you backwoods upstart."

Tom could barely restrain a smile at James' bold language as he stood flaunting his courage so close behind his burly friend.

"I will indeed mind, Mr. James Purdie, and I swear unless you give me fair reason, I will not only run but, by gad, I'll beat this mountainous friend of yours so badly that he'll be the laughingstock of the whole town."

There came an angry yelp from the blacksmith as he leapt forward. Then the high whine of the long whip. Tom felt a stinging pain streak down his face and across his back. He ducked. Half blinded by the blow, he fell forward. Once more came the whine of the whip over his head. This time it struck him across his shoulders. Throwing his hands over his head to protect himself, Tom staggered to his feet, but, catching his foot in a root, he was thrown forward and lay helplessly trapped.

The huge man above him grunted in brute rage. He waited for the terrible sound of the whip. But it did not come. Instead, Tom heard a deep, angry voice call out from the woods behind the blacksmith.

"Stop. Stop that, you fool. You could kill the boy."

Tom hardly dared to move. But that voice. That voice. Tom knew it well, but he could not tell now in the confusion whose it was.

Staggering to his feet as best he could, Tom leaned heavily against the trunk of a pine tree. It was hard to make out anything clearly in the darkness, but the blacksmith had retreated, dropping his whip, and raised his arms slowly in the air as he watched a dark figure come forward quickly from the trees across the road. A three-cornered hat, pulled far down over his forehead, partially concealed the newcomer's face, but there was no mistaking the gleam of a small pistol held firmly in the stranger's right hand.

"Now I think we've had enough of this business. Get out of here, you two." The man wheeled about suddenly, almost touching the cowering James, who had retreated as quickly as possible behind the largest tree he could find. "Filthy rats that you are—get out." The man's voice rose angrily. "Get out. If I find either of you daring to so much as speak to this boy again"—the man flourished his pistol in Tom's direction with exquisite elegance—"well, there's always a way to put a stop to things I find annoying."

Two shadows, one heavy and dark, the other thin and mincing, hurried quickly down the road and were instantly swallowed up by the night.

The figure on the other side of the road turned toward Tom with a low chuckle.

"Well, Tom," said the stranger, uncocking the pistol and slipping it into his coat pocket, "do you know me?"

It took Tom a moment to collect himself. He spoke haltingly, only half believing what he said.

"Mr. Valentine! It's you!"

"Eh, it's me all right. Are you that surprised to see me again?"

"Well—well, I can't say I'd expected you, but I can say I'm mighty glad you came when you did."

Mr. Valentine stepped across the road nimbly and came up to Tom, looking down at his ankle. "Have they hurt you?"

"No, not really." Tom winced at the sudden pain in his ankle as he tried to take a step forward. He realized then that he must have twisted it more severely than he had thought. Mr. Valentine knelt beside him. His long fingers examined Tom's leg and ankle.

"There's nothing broken. Try to walk on it."

Tom tried and managed to take a few steps forward, and then he sank to the ground. Mr. Valentine stood over him for a moment looking down. Then, pulling up the tails of his elegant coat, joined Tom, and the two sat silent for a moment.

Tom was too bewildered by all that had just happened even to ask questions. Then he began hesitantly.

"Mr. Valentine, Mr. Valentine, why, why are you here? How did you know this was going to happen to me? Why, why is young James so anxious that I should not enter this race. I don't understand anything." Tom lifted a puzzled face to his companion. Even in the darkness, he could make out the familiar half smile twisting across the thin lips.

"It's all a dirty, stinking affair, Tom." Mr. Valentine spoke quietly and almost gently. "As far as I can make out, James Purdie has money troubles. He's borrowed too much for the horse races, and he's afraid he'll not be able to pay. So he cooked up this little plan of betting again on something he felt sure he could not lose. I just happen to know that, this time, instead of betting on horses, he's bet on a human race. In other words, he felt so sure his friend Jake here would win tomorrow, that he thought he could pay off all his debts if he could get somebody to bet with him. He did. Somebody else felt just as sure you would win."

"Me!" Tom gasped. "Somebody bet money on me?"

"Yes," Mr. Valentine continued. "Somebody must have bet a lot of money on you. Now, I don't know who it was, and I don't think we ever will, but at first young James thought he was quite safe. You've been cooped up in that print shop for a year. You've put on weight, if you'll excuse me for being so personal, and, well, until I heard that you've been training hard for the past two weeks, I would have said that you were not much of a bet, either."

"Bet!" Tom could hardly believe what he had just heard. "You mean to say that James Purdie bet on Jake just as he would on a race horse?"

"I'm afraid so, Tom. There's no telling what young Purdie will do for money, and besides, it's not the first time it's been done in the town. To be honest, Tom, this race from the college to the Capitol is not the innocent affair it would appear. There's a group here that would bet on anything, whether it's a horse race, a cockfight, or a bunch of young lads running down the Duke of Gloucester Street. Indeed, there were odds for and against you in the taverns, just as if you were to run at the race track tomorrow. And I want to tell you that you were a strong favorite, too." Mr. Valentine couldn't hide a low chuckle.

Men betting on him as if he were an animal! Tom felt sick and disgusted. "So that's why James was so anxious that I should not race," he said almost to himself.

"Yes," Mr. Valentine said thoughtfully. "And I heard about it only by chance this evening, and—well"—there was a long pause—"Tom, you did me quite a turn, you know, saying I was your friend and not mentioning your purse."

"My purse!" Tom gasped. In the excitement, he had forgotten. He questioned, "Then you did take it from me that first day?"

There was another long silence after that. The tall pines whispered together overhead in the soft evening wind. There were tiny rustlings among the dry pine needles as little night animals scuttled to safety.

"Yes, Tom, I took it. And if you knew how many times I've cursed myself for it since then. You could never understand, Tom, but it's just—it's just that that's the way I live. If I see a purse lying, as yours was when it fell out of your bundle onto the street—well, I take it. It's mine, Tom. That's all there is to it. Sometimes I have to work harder, of course; slip a hand in an unsuspecting victim's pocket or lift a window at night, although, of course, I don't like that kind of a job—too liable to be caught."

Tom had never known what punishment Mr. Valentine received for the attempted robbery of the post office. Somehow, he had not wanted to know, and Mr. Purdie had not told him.

"He's quite a man, that master of yours," Mr. Valentine said, looking down at Tom. "Did you ever hear what he did?"

Tom shook his head. "He interceded for me, and I got off after only a few months in that stinking jail. They made me promise I'd never return to bother the good people of Williamsburg again, said it would go very badly for me if I did. But—here I am. Thought there would be a fair on St. George's Day, as usual, and of course, I can't stay away from a fair, Tom. That's how I heard about the race and, of course, about you."

Tom didn't move. He couldn't speak. He was too confused about this man. He didn't know how he felt. Perhaps he felt sorry for him. Perhaps, in some strange way, he even liked him. Mr. Valentine stirred and rose slowly to his feet.

"Good night," he said. "You can walk home by yourself all

right?" Tom nodded. "Good luck, and I'm sorry about the race and that ankle."

Mr. Valentine held out his hand. Tom hesitated, then somehow he couldn't help taking it. His hand went out to the other. As they met, he felt something heavy and warm pass into his palm. Then the dark figure was gone, vanishing as quickly as the first night Tom had met him.

Tom looked down. There were three coins, three golden doubloons! Every penny Mr. Valentine had taken from him one year before.

CHAPTER 19

Tom hobbled back down the road and crept into the shop as best he could with his now badly swollen ankle. Milly followed along quietly behind him.

"She seems to know I've been hurt," Tom thought, looking down at the little ball of white jogging along by his side now. "What a comfort you've been to me," he whispered as he struggled up the steep little stairs to his room. "But you shouldn't have been off chasing rabbits tonight and let those bullies get so near."

Tom smiled at the very thought of the tiny dog attempting to protect him from Jake and his cruel whip. This reminded him of the sore on his back, which ached now, and raising his hand to his face, Tom could feel another swelling across his right cheek.

"The dirty black cad. Now I'll never be able to race him and beat him, and think how young Purdie will crow then." This thought hurt almost more than the ankle and the great red welts on his cheek and back put together.

When he had lighted his candle, Tom sank onto the bed and drove his hand deep in his pocket, bringing out the coins Mr. Valentine had given him. "But at least I have this to send her." Tom's anger soon changed to happiness at the thought that he would now be able to return, not part, but all of the money his mother had given him.

Throwing his clothes off, he climbed wearily into his bed and was about to blow out the candle that stood nearby on his writing desk, when he noticed Milly sitting up very straight on her rug by the door.

"What's the trouble now, small one?"

Milly gave a short bark, and there were footsteps in the shop down below. Before Tom could get himself disentangled from his covers, James Purdie stood in the doorway. His face was streaked with dirt. His eyes were wild. Was that a faint red welt down the side of his cheek, too? Tom wasn't sure.

"Tom, Tom," the boy gasped. "Tom, I know I should not come here. That man warned me not to come near you. But I had to. You must not run tomorrow. Please, Tom, promise me."

James put his hand into his coat pocket and pulled out several coins. "Look, Tom," he went on, almost gasping in his fear and haste, "I know you only wanted to sell the buckles if you won them. Here, here's what you would have gotten from the silversmith or anyone else. Tom, will you take these, please, and not race tomorrow?"

The slight rise of pity Tom had felt when James entered disappeared quickly as he understood what he was up to. The dirty, filthy little cad had come here to try and buy Tom off, to try and bribe him with money not to run tomorrow. Putting his hand on the edge of his bed, Tom attempted to get up, but he fell back. His ankle hurt too much. He hesitated, and as he did so a sudden thought came to him. Having been startled by James' sudden appearance, he had completely forgotten that nobody but Mr. Valentine knew anything about his bad ankle. James must be quite unaware that, money or no money, Tom could not possibly enter the race tomorrow.

Slowly Tom's anger turned to amusement. Leaning casually on his elbow, he looked up at the boy standing beside him. "How much am I offered?" he asked coolly.

"Twenty shillings, and you promise you will not race tomorrow."

"Twenty shillings," he thought. "Just right for a new doll for Milly." He turned over casually in bed, being careful that the covers kept his injured ankle well concealed.

Tom yawned. "All right, James," he drawled slowly. "If it will really make you happy, you can leave the twenty shillings on the table," he said, closing his eyes. "I'm tired."

"Of course, you must be after everything that's happened tonight." James sounded foolishly eager. "I'm sorry about tonight. I'm really sorry."

There was a clink of silver as James obeyed the order, the shuffle of feet on the narrow stairs, then the sound of the shop door closing, and Tom knew that James was gone.

Turning over quickly in his bed, Tom reached for the little pile of money on the table. He counted it carefully, twenty shillings, sure enough. Then he got up and put it in a small metal box with the money that Mr. Valentine had returned to him.

"Not a bad night for a poor printer's apprentice lying flat on his back with a sprained ankle," he thought happily to himself as he hobbled back to his bed and blew out the candle.

CHAPTER 20

It was the fifteenth of May, 1776, a clear, fresh day with a blue sky and soft white clouds like great balloons afloat in the air. As the sun rose higher, its heat brought the smell of boxwood, strong and sweet from the gardens.

"Tom," said Mr. Purdie, walking slowly, leaning heavily on Tom's arm. "Tom, I think we are about to attend what may prove to be the most important session ever held in our Capitol, and there have been some pretty important meetings there, too."

The older man breathed heavily, stopping often to rest. Tom looked anxiously at his master, wondering if he should be walking even the short distance from his house to the Capitol, for Mr. Purdie seemed, even to Tom's inexperienced eyes, to be failing very fast, although no mention had ever been made between them as to what his illness might be.

"I know, sir. They say the committee will really bring in the resolution today."

"Independence. Who would have thought, Tom"—Mr. Purdie spoke slowly—"who would have thought even a year ago that we would declare ourselves independent from the mother country? But I swear, it's not our doing. They forced us to want this. Why, Tom, you can't imagine how loyal we were to Lord Botetourt, and he to us, for that matter. If only they had sent us another governor like him, instead of that arrogant Dunmore, we might have patched up the troubles."

Tom couldn't help smiling a bit. He knew full well that Mr. Purdie did not really believe this any more than he himself did. "Do you really believe that Patrick Henry would have talked of patching things up?"

"No, maybe you're right, boy." Mr. Purdie spoke almost to himself. "Perhaps, perhaps things had gone too far. Yes, unjust taxation, bloodshed, and being declared in a state of revolt by the Crown—yes, that's too much."

Tom looked up at the beautiful Capitol building as if he had never seen it before, although he had delivered the Gazette to the clerk's office every Friday for an entire year. He had never, however, been in any of the chambers. Now, as he and Mr. Purdie were shown to a seat in the gallery at the back of the former Burgesses' chamber, Tom could hardly believe that he was really inside. Mr. Purdie, sitting down slowly, motioned for him to stand behind the chair.

"I may not be able to last through the whole session," he whispered "Be ready to help me, Tom."

Tom felt a deep sense of gravity as he looked about this room knowing it was here that the men chosen by free election had sat to make the laws of Virginia during the seventy-six years that Williamsburg had been capital of the colony. The room was not large. Along both sides were the benches for the burgesses, and at the end of the room was the great covered chair for the president. There was a table covered with a heavy green table carpet for the clerks and a branching brass chandelier to light the sessions that lasted late into the night.

The seats were beginning to fill up now. As the men entered, Tom found that he knew many of them: Mr. Thomas Nelson, Jr., Mr. Meriweather Smith, and, of course, Mr. Robert Carter Nicholas. At the clerk's table sat Mr. Tazewell, ready to record what was said.

Suddenly there was a stir at the door, and the tall, lanky figure came in. Patrick Henry! Tom felt himself alert, anxious, and listening. There was something so alive, so eager about the man. He walked jerkily to his seat and sat, several papers strewn across his bony knees, as if so occupied with his own thoughts that he scarcely noticed the presence of the other members.

The door opened once more, and the chairman, Mr. Edmund Pendleton, entered. Tom had seen the man only as he drove in his carriage to and from the Capitol, but never closely before. He was struck by how handsome he was as he walked quickly to the president's chair.

So the great meeting was called to order, and before Tom quite realized what was happening, Mr. Cary was on his feet and, at the bidding of the president, reading. Tom listened, scarcely daring to breathe. The light flooded in through the great round windows at the end of the chamber, slanting across Mr. Cary's face as he read, and there was no other sound in the room but the endless buzzing of flies at the window.

At last Mr. Cary's clear, strong voice concluded: "'Resolved: That the delegates appointed to represent this colony in general Congress be instructed to propose, to that respectable body, to declare the united colonies free and independent states'"—Mr. Cary stopped to reread, "' . . . to declare the united colonies free and independent states'"—"'absolved from all allegiance to or dependence upon the Crown or Parliament of Great Britain.

"'Resolved: That a committee be appointed to prepare a Declaration of Rights and such a plan of government as will be most likely to maintain peace and order in this colony and secure substantial and equal liberty to her people.'"

The resolutions were passed unanimously, and the word spread like fire! Already, as Mr. Purdie walked from the gallery, the walled yard of the Capitol was filled with eager men and women. Tom, trying in vain to clear a path for Mr. Purdie, suddenly felt a hand on his shoulder. Turning quickly, he saw the distressed face of old Mr. Goodfellow. Tom knew him well as the custodian, the man in charge of the Capitol building and the man responsible for raising and lowering the flag each day.

"Tom, Tom," the little man fairly wept, "come, Tom, you must help me. The flag is stuck. You're young and nimble. They're shouting to have down with the British flag and up with their new one, and I can't budge either."

Tom saw Mr. Purdie safely though the crowded door and out into the yard. Then, turning, he pushed his way back into the building and hurried up the stairs to the tower. There stood Mr. Goodfellow, his old fingers shaking, his wig all askew, and great drops of sweat standing out all over his pointed chin. Looking up, Tom saw the trouble, and with a leap soon clambered to a place where he could unfasten the badly snarled rope. Old Goodfellow tugged. Tom dropped to the balcony. Down came the flag of Great Britain, and up went the new Union flag of the United Colonies!

A great shout rose from below: "Hurrah! Hurrah for the new flag of liberty!"

"Hurrah for freedom from tyranny!"

"Let us cry liberty, independence, and freedom!"

Tom watched from his perch high above the wild crowd. Hats flew in the air. Ladies tossed tiny lace handkerchiefs over their heads, and small children did cartwheels without understanding the reasons for rejoicing.

"Freedom!"

"Good night, King George!"

"Farewell, unjust taxation!"

"Let us cry liberty!"

"Hurrah, hurrah, and hurrah!"

Tom turned to look up at the new flag again. He swallowed hard, for all of a sudden he felt far away, above, detached, and not part of this cheering throng. He felt he must be something, just resting there for a moment in the sky high above all the wild yelling and excitement. High, high above like a single bird that might have flown over and watched this strange demonstration.

The flag with the thirteen red and white stripes waved against the clear blue sky, and far away, as if only pasted against the curving sky, were white clouds, puffed and round, with the red and white stripes curling and flowing in front of them.

The celebration lasted all of that day and on into the next, with the soldiers parading at Waller's Grove, and Brigadier General Lewis reviewing them. The fifes and drums played, and there were many toasts:

"To the American Independence."

"To the Grand Congress of the United States."

The most heartfelt of all was "To General George Washington, and victory to the American arms!"

Tom went to sleep at last with the sound of the Roman candles, the rockets, and the firecrackers pounding all night in his ears.

CHAPTER 21

"But, Mr. Purdie," Tom said, looking at the first page of the Gazette, all neatly set up and ready for the press, "what is this? It's all different."

Mr. Purdie smiled happily. "Eh, Tom, it's all different. And pray why should we have the seal of Virginia as the heading of our paper with the old motto which proclaims us as one-fifth of the British Empire when we are that no longer? I mean, if the Congress up in Philadelphia joins with us in our declaration of Independence? No, Tom, that is all over now, I truly hope, and until we can get a new masthead, I have decided to use this simple box."

THE THIRTEEN UNITED COLONIES

UNITED WE STAND, DIVIDED WE FALL.

"That's wonderful, Mr. Purdie." Tom ran his hand over the new type. "The thirteen united colonies." He was quiet a moment, thinking. Then he asked, "Mr. Purdie, do you think that now that Virginia has directed its delegates to the Congress in Philadelphia to vote for independence that the other colonies will follow us?"

"There's no telling, Tom. Maybe they will and maybe they won't, but I hope so," Mr. Purdie answered slowly. "Of course, we couldn't be independent if the other twelve colonies decided they didn't want to be also. We've got the best men we could have up there in Philadelphia, and as soon as they receive the instructions to introduce the resolutions for independence, well, if Mr. Jefferson, Mr. Lee, Mr. George Wythe, and the others can't persuade the whole Congress to declare independence, I don't know who can."

"Oh, I hope they do. They must. Surely the colony of Massachusetts will follow them, and Pennsylvania. Do you think New York will vote for it?"

"Tom, I don't know how things are going up there. All we can do is be glad Virginia has taken the step; now maybe since we're prepared to break with the mother country, the others will be willing to follow. But come, we must get this Gazette out. Put that first page in the press. If there's any one of our subscribers who doesn't know the great news, we'd better get it to them in a hurry."

Tom carried the heavy case in which the type was set to the press, fitted it onto the carriage, inked the type and particularly the new heading carefully, and put the damp paper in place. Then he began the long day's work, "twisting the devil's tail" with a will, for the news that he printed was good news.

From that day on, the work in the shop grew heavier and heavier, for it seemed as if each week brought some news of great importance hurrying from the Capitol that required special work and long hours of typesetting for Mr. Purdie. Tom took charge of the news from overseas, letters from London, the notices to the troops, and reports on the fighting up north.

On the twelfth of June came the great Declaration of Rights, written by the brilliant George Mason. It was voted on and passed by the convention, and Mr. Purdie had to put out a postscript that took all night to set up and print. Tom read eagerly:

THAT ALL MEN ARE BY NATURE EQUALLY FREE
AND INDEPENDENT AND HAVE CERTAIN INHERENT
RIGHTS******NAMELY THE ENJOYMENT OF LIFE
AND LIBERTY . . . ALL POWER IS VESTED IN AND
CONSEQUENTLY DERIVED FROM THE PEOPLE.

"These are rights that nobody can ever take from us now, Tom." Mr. Purdie read the words over and over before he started to set them. "We've never had anything like this before. Do you really understand what this Bill of Rights means, Tom?" Mr. Purdie put his composing stick down and looked earnestly at Tom standing beside him. "Do you really understand that, if this Bill of Rights is accepted and adopted by whatever government these colonies create, it means that every man in the colonies is born free and independent? That means no government can give us our freedom or take it away from us. The English Parliament can do that if it pleases, but we, by the Bill of Rights, are just born free men."

Mr. Purdie stopped a moment, looking searchingly at his apprentice, as if to see whether he truly understood the significance of what he had just said. "That's a wonderful thing, Tom." Mr. Purdie took up his composing stick and started to pick out the letters he needed from the type case in front of him. "It's a wonderful thing, that is, if we and those who come after us will live up to it."

The Bill of Rights was soon followed on the twenty-ninth of June by the completion of a constitution for Virginia. It began with a statement of the wrongs done the colony by the king and Parliament and proceeded to outline the new government.

It wasn't long after the adoption of the new constitution that Patrick Henry, who had retired from the Army, was made governor and installed in the palace. There were those who still thought of the new governor as a backwoodsman and wondered how he could assume the dignity necessary for his new office. But their fears were soon quieted when Governor Henry bought a new wig to go with a fine suit of black clothes he'd had made for himself, and rode out in the evenings wrapped about in a brilliant red cape.

These were important times in the little capital city of Virginia, but there were few who did not realize how much more important was the news from the Congress working through the sweltering summer up north in Philadelphia. Post riders came and went, and still there was no report that the Congress would accept the Virginian delegate's resolutions for a Declaration of Independence from the mother country.

News came one day that July first had been set as the final date for the resolutions to be voted on. But the first of July came and went, and still nothing was definite. The people of Williamsburg waited. They waited with their demand for independence declared. They waited with their own Bill of Rights written, their new constitution already in motion, and their new governor in office.

Then at last it arrived. The news came! The resolutions had been passed. The Declaration of Independence had been adopted! The order went out that this Declaration of Independence should be read aloud to the people of each county in the commonwealth. And so it was in Williamsburg, and Tom gathered in front of the courthouse with the rest of the townsfolk, eager, tense, waiting. He knew well what this moment meant. He, too, had waited for the news with the others. He, too, had read and reread every report Mr. Purdie had received from the Congress, but this was what he, like the others, had been waiting for.

He listened, hardly stirring, scarcely breathing in the heat of the bright July sun, as the news was read; the declaration that the thirteen colonies of America had voted to declare themselves independent and free from the mother country—Great Britain!

Tom cheered with the rest. He was hoarse with cheering. His hat was trampled and ruined as he hurled it with the others high in the air, rejoicing.

At last, when the soldiers began their parading, when the volley of musketry began banging, and the cannons set in place as the magazine started their deep-throated booming, Tom hurried back to the shop.

"Mr. Purdie, Mr. Purdie," he called. The shop was quite empty. There was no answer, but Mr. Purdie was there when he left for the courthouse, for he had told Tom to go for him, to listen carefully to what was said, and report the proceedings to him. Tom had scarcely been gone two hours. He was suddenly worried.

Hurrying upstairs, he looked to see if the older man had gone there to rest, but only the echo of Tom's footsteps answered his calls. Running downstairs once more, he made his way as quickly as possible through the great crowd of people pushing along the Duke of Gloucester Street, shoving into the Raleigh

Tavern, and filling up the sidewalk outside the King's Arms. Tom flung open the door at the Purdie's.

"Mr. Purdie." His voice rose in spite of his effort to be calm.

"Sh, sh, Tom," Miss Peachy said quietly from upstairs.

"There's nothing wrong? He's not sick?" Tom started up the stairs.

"Tom, Tom, come here." Tom heard Mr. Purdie's voice.

"Oh, there you are. Then you came back here to the house. I was afraid, I thought . . ." Tom's voice trailed off as he saw Mr. Purdie lying on the high, curtained bed, his wig off, and his face as white as the pillow on which he lay.

"Mr. Purdie!" Tom almost whispered. "Are you, are you—"

"Yes, Tom, I'm afraid I am sick, sicker than I had thought." Mr. Purdie closed his eyes for a moment.

Tom felt himself go hot and then icy cold. No, no, nothing could really happen to Mr. Purdie. The thoughts whirled in his head. Then the older man stirred. Lifting himself slightly, he half sat up.

"Now, now, that's better." His tired face had more color. His eyes had more life. His lips were no longer that terrible blue.

"Tom, Tom, I can't come now. It's up to you. The Declaration of Independence must be set up and printed, not only because it's—it's an order of Congress, but because it's the most important thing that has ever happened." He stopped. Miss Peachy had come into the room and sat quietly on the edge of the bed.

"Don't, Alexander, don't tire yourself." She took her husband's hand and sat stroking it.

"No, no, Peachy, but I must explain to Tom." Mr. Purdie's eyes closed again for a moment, then he continued. His voice fell to a faint whisper. "This is the most important thing we ever printed in our Gazette, Tom, and it's up to you to get started setting it up. I'll come when I can."

Tom gasped. "Me, me, sir?" He could hardly believe what he had just heard. "You want me to set the whole Declaration of Independence alone, all by myself, without even your being there to proofread it?"

"Yes, Tom, you can do it if I am not able to get there. And when you are through, you'll be—" Mr. Purdie hesitated a moment, looking at Tom. "You'll be Tom Cartwright, a printer, not an apprentice anymore."

For a moment, Mr. Purdie's eyes seemed to have that old twinkle and his mouth the old smile that Tom had trusted since the first night he had seen his new master through the shop window.

"Go—hurry, Tom, and God bless you." The sick man fell back and held out his hand. Tom grasped it, but he could not speak.

Hardly conscious of the shoving, the shouting, or the loud cannons that were still booming at the magazine, Tom made his way to the shop as quickly as the wild crowd would let him.

He entered hurriedly and, turning, locked the door behind him. There must be no interruptions now. He took off his coat and put on his long printer's apron. Then slowly he went to the type cases. Grasping the composing stick in his left hand, he reached for the capital W, and with trembling fingers began:

WHEN IN THE COURSE OF HUMAN EVENTS IT BECOMES NECESSARY FOR ONE PEOPLE TO DISSOLVE THE POLITICAL BANDS WHICH HAVE CONNECTED THEM WITH ANOTHER . . .